Michael Ende

The Night of Wishes

or, The Satanarchaeolidealcohellish Notion Potion

Translated from the German by
Heike Schwarzbauer and Rick Takvorian

Pictures by Regina Kehn

THE NEW YORK REVIEW CHILDREN'S COLLECTION
New York

Translators' Dedication:
To Nick and the pink sofa

THIS IS A NEW YORK REVIEW BOOK
PUBLISHED BY THE NEW YORK REVIEW OF BOOKS
435 Hudson Street, New York, NY 10014
www.nyrb.com

First published in German in 1989 as *Der satanarchäolügenialkohöllische
Wunschpunsch* by K. Thienemanns Verlag, Stuttgart–Vienna

Library of Congress Cataloging-in-Publication Data
Names: Ende, Michael, author. | Kehn, Regina, illustrator. | Schwarzbauer,
  Heike, translator. | Takvorian, Rick, translator.
Title: The night of wishes : or, The satanarchaeolidealcohellish notion
  potion / by Michael Ende ; illustrated by Regina Kehn ; translated from
  the German by Heike Schwarzbauer and by Rick Takvorian.
Other titles: Satanarchäolügenialkohöllische Wunschpunsch. English
Description: New York : New York Review Books, [2017] | Series: New
  York Review Children's Collection
Identifiers: LCCN 2017013742 | ISBN 9781681371887 (hardback)
Subjects: LCSH: Magic—Fiction. | Wizards—Fiction. | Occult fiction. |
  Humorous stories. | BISAC: JUVENILE FICTION / Fantasy & Magic. |
  JUVENILE FICTION / Holidays & Celebrations / Other, Non-Religious.
Classification: LCC PT2665.N27 S2613 2017 | DDC 833/.914—dc23
LC record available at https://lccn.loc.gov/2017013742

ISBN 978-1-68137-188-7
Available as an electronic book; ISBN 978-1-68137-248-8

Printed in the United States of America on acid-free paper.
10 9 8 7 6 5 4 3 2 1

Pitch blackness had settled much earlier than usual over this, the last afternoon of the year. Black clouds darkened the sky and a blizzard had been raging through the Dead Park for hours.

Nothing was stirring within the Villa Nightmare—except for the flickering shadow of the fire, its green flames burning in the hearth and casting an eerie glow over the sorcerer's laboratory.

The works of the pendulum clock above the mantelpiece rattled to life. It was a cuckoo clock of sorts, except that its elaborate mechanism consisted of a sore thumb being struck by a hammer.

"Ouch!" it said. "Ouch!—Ouch!—Ouch!—Ouch!"

So it was five o'clock.

Normally the striking of the clock put Shadow Sorcery Minister Beelzebub Preposteror in an exceptionally good mood, but on this particular New Year's Eve he cast a rather woebegone glance in its direction. Dismissing it with a listless wave of his hand, he wrapped himself in the smoke of his pipe and brooded away with downcast brow. He knew that big trouble lay ahead. At midnight at the latest—with the coming of the New Year.

The sorcerer sat in a spacious armchair which had been built out of coffin planks four hundred years ago by a handy vampire. The cushions were made from the pelts of werewolves and had, admittedly, become a little shabby over the years. This piece of furniture was a family heirloom and Preposteror cherished it, although he was for the most part rather progressive and moved with the times—at least as far as his profession was concerned.

The pipe he smoked was in the shape of a small skull whose green glass eyes lit up with every puff. Little clouds of smoke took all manner of curious shapes in the air: numbers and equations, coiling snakes, bats, little ghosts, but mainly question marks.

Beelzebub Preposteror uttered a deep sigh, rose to his feet, and began pacing back and forth in his laboratory. He would be held accountable, of that he was certain. But whom would he have to answer to? And what could he present in his defense? And above all, would they buy his excuses?

His tall, bony figure was clothed in a pleated dressing gown of bilious green silk (bilious green being the Shadow Sorcery Minister's favorite color). His head was small and bald and looked somehow shriveled, like a withered apple. On his hooked nose perched a pair of huge, black-rimmed glasses, with glittering lenses as thick as magnifying glasses, which enlarged his eyes to an unnatural degree. His ears stood out like handles on a pot and his mouth was as thin as if it had been sliced into his face with a razor. All in all, he was not exactly the kind of guy you would trust at first glance. Yet this did not bother Preposteror in the least; he had never been a particularly sociable character. Given the choice, he preferred his own company and working in seclusion.

At one point he stopped pacing and pensively scratched his bald dome.

"If nothing else, potion No. 92 absolutely must get finished today," he muttered. "I hope that cursed tomcat won't get in the way."

He stepped toward the fireplace.

On an iron tripod there stood amid the green flames a glass cauldron, wherein simmered a certain brew, which looked rather revolting: black as tar and icky as snail slime. Critically stirring the stuff with a wand of mountain crystal, Preposteror let his thoughts wander as he listened to the whining and wuthering of the blizzard which shook the shutters.

Alas, the brew would have to bubble for quite a while still before it was finished cooking and properly transmutated.

As soon as the potion was done, it would render a completely tasteless solution which could be mixed in with every sort of food and drink. All those who partook of it would henceforth firmly believe that everything that Preposteror produced served the progress of humanity. The sorcerer intended to deliver it to all the supermarkets in the city shortly after New Year's Day, to be sold under the name Mr. Pick-Me-Up's Diet.

But he hadn't gotten that far yet. These things took time—and *that* was the fly in the ointment.

The Shadow Sorcery Minister put down his pipe and let his gaze wander through the semidarkness of the laboratory. The reflection of the green fire shuddered against the mountains of old and new books containing all the mixtures and formulas which Preposteror needed for his experiments. Test tubes, glasses, bottles, and spiraling coils glistened mysteriously from the darkest corners of the room, their multicolored liquids rising and falling, dripping and steaming. Tiny lamps blinked continually, punctuating the low humming and beeping of computers and electrical appliances. In a dark recess,

luminous globes of red and blue levitated and descended in a soundless and steady rhythm, and smoke swirled within a crystal jar, forming a glimmering spectral flower at regular intervals.

As we have already mentioned, Preposteror was definitely an up-to-date, state-of-the-art sorcerer; in fact, in some respects he was well ahead of his time.

But he had fallen hopelessly behind schedule with his deadlines.

A low coughing startled him.

He whipped around.

Someone was sitting in the big old armchair.

Aha, he thought, here we go. Pull yourself together!

Now, a sorcerer—and especially one of Preposteror's ilk—is certainly used to all manner of unearthly creatures appearing in his presence, frequently unannounced and uninvited; but they are usually ghosts carrying their heads under their arms, or villains with three eyes and six hands, or fire-breathing dragons, or other such monstrosities. None of this would have frightened the Shadow Sorcery Minister in the least; he was familiar with this world. It was, in fact, the daily or nightly company he kept.

This visitor, however, was completely different. He looked as normal as any man on the street—almost frighteningly normal. And that was what made Preposteror lose his composure.

The man was wearing a proper black coat, a stiff black hat on his head, and black gloves; a black briefcase was poised on his knees. His face betrayed no emotion whatsoever and was very pale, almost white. His colorless eyes bulged slightly and he stared without blinking. He had no eyelids.

Preposteror pulled himself together and approached the visitor. "Who are you? What do you want?"

The visitor took his time. He stared back at his interlocutor for a while with cold pop eyes before answering in a flat voice, "Have I the pleasure of addressing Shadow Sorcery Minister Beelzebub Preposteror?"

"You have indeed. —Well?"

"Please allow me to introduce myself."

Without rising from his chair, the visitor tipped his hat slightly, and for a split second two small reddish bumps, which looked like pustules, were visible on his smooth white skull.

"My name is Maggot—Maledictus Maggot, if you please."

The sorcerer was still determined not to be impressed.

"And what gives you the right to infringe upon my privacy?"

"Oh," said Mr. Maggot without so much as a smile, "if you will allow me to say so, dear sir, you of all people should not ask so foolish a question."

Preposteror knitted his fingers so tightly that his knuckles cracked. "You don't come from . . . ?"

"Quite right," confirmed the gentleman, "from there," simultaneously pointing downward with his thumb.

Preposteror swallowed dryly and said nothing.

His guest continued, "I have come at the personal behest of His Hellish Excellency, your most worthy benefactor."

The sorcerer attempted to feign a pleased smile, but his teeth suddenly seemed to be glued together. Only with great difficulty was he able to stutter, "What an honor."

"That it is, dear sir," answered the visitor. "I have been sent by the Minister of Pitch Darkness himself, His Excellency Beelzebub, whose name you are permitted to enjoy the undeserved honor of bearing. My unworthy self is merely an executive body of the lowest category. Once I have carried out my mission to the satisfaction of His Excellency, I can hope to soon be promoted—perhaps even to head of a spooking department."

"Congratulations, Mr. Maggot," stammered Preposteror. "And what might your mission be?" His face had taken on a slightly greenish tinge.

"I have come here in an exclusively official capacity," Mr. Maggot declared, "as a bailiff, if you will."

The sorcerer had to clear his throat; his voice sounded thick. "But what, by all the black holes in the universe, do you want with me? To foreclose? There must be some mistake."

"We shall see," said Mr. Maggot.

He extracted a document from his black briefcase and held it out to Preposteror. "You are no doubt familiar with this contract, most honored Shadow Sorcery Minister. You yourself in person entered into it with my boss and signed it with your own hand. It states that you shall be granted extraordinary powers in this century by your benefactor—quite extraordinary powers indeed—over all of nature and all your fellow mortals. It also states, however, that each year you are obliged to render extinct, by means direct or indirect, ten species of animal, be it butterfly, fish, or mammal. Furthermore, five rivers are to be polluted, or one and the same river five times. Moreover, at least ten thousand trees are to die off, and so on and so forth, down to the final clauses: each year to bring at least one new plague into the world by which humans or animals or both together shall perish. And lastly: to manipulate the climate of your country in such a way that the seasons go out of kilter and either droughts or floods occur. You have met only half your obligations this past year, most honored sir. My boss finds this very, very regrettable. He is—if I may be so graphic—annoyed. You know what it means when His Excellency gets annoyed. Do you have anything to state by way of rejoinder?"

Preposteror, who had repeatedly attempted to interrupt his visitor, now burst out, "But the old year isn't over yet! Shades of dioxin, it's only New Year's Eve. I've still got until midnight."

Mr. Maggot fixed him with a lidless gaze. "By all means, and do you intend"—here he cast a quick glance at the clock—"to make up the difference in these few remaining hours, dear sir? Do you indeed?"

"Of course!" croaked Preposteror. But then he hung his head and murmured meekly, "No, it's impossible."

The visitor rose and approached the wall near the fireplace, where all the Shadow Sorcery Minister's diplomas hung neatly framed. Preposteror, like most of his peers, attached the greatest amount of importance to such titles. One diploma, for example, said B.A.B.A. (Brotherhood of the Academy of Black Arts), another DR. H.C. (Doctor Horroris Causa), a third PR. A.I. (Professor of Applied Infamy), and yet another A.B.C. (Association of the Brocken Council), and so on.

"Now, listen here," said Preposteror, "let's be reasonable. It's really not a question of bad will; I've got more than enough of that, I can assure you."

"Really?" asked Mr. Maggot.

The sorcerer wiped the cold sweat from his bald dome with a handkerchief. "I'll catch up with everything as soon as possible. His Excellency can rest assured. Please tell him so."

"Catch up?" asked Mr. Maggot.

"Damnation," cried Preposteror, "quite simply, circumstances have arisen which have made it impossible for me to fulfill my contractual obligations on time. Just a slight extension and everything will be all right again."

"Circumstances?" repeated Mr. Maggot, all the while continuing to peruse the diplomas in a rather uninterested manner. "What circumstances?"

The sorcerer stepped closer to him and urgently addressed his stiff black hat. "Presumably you know yourself that what I have accomplished in the last few years went far beyond my contractual obligations."

Mr. Maggot turned and treated Preposteror's face to his opaque stare. "Let's say it was satisfactory—no more, no less."

The Shadow Sorcery Minister was starting to babble as his panic increased, until he, all in a muddle, finally blurted out, "You just can't conduct a campaign of destruction without the enemy noticing it sooner or later. It is precisely because of my special achievements that nature is now beginning to defend itself. It is preparing to retaliate—it just doesn't know yet against whom. Of course, the first ones to rebel were the elemental spirits: the gnomes, dwarfs, nymphs, and elves; they are the most clever. It took an enormous amount of time and effort to catch and render harmless all those who had found us out and could stand in the way of our plans. Unfortunately, they can't be destroyed, since they are immortal, but I was able to lock them up and paralyze them completely with my magic powers. By the way, it is a remarkable collection—if you care to see for yourself, it is out in the hallway, Mr. Slug . . ."

"Maggot," said the visitor, without taking him up on his offer.

"What? Oh, ahem, yes, of course, Mr. Maggot. I beg your pardon."

The sorcerer managed a nervous giggle. "The remaining elemental spirits have gotten cold feet and fled to the four corners of the earth. So we are rid of them for good.

"But meanwhile, even the animals have become suspicious. They have called a High Council and decided to send secret observers to every point of the compass in order to find the root of all evil. And unfortunately, I have been host to one of these spies for about a year. A small tomcat. Fortunately, he is not exactly what you'd call bright. He's asleep at the moment, in case you'd like to look in on him. Truth be known, he sleeps a great deal—and not just because he is a lazy puss."

Here the sorcerer grinned. "I've made certain that he doesn't notice what I'm really up to. He doesn't even realize that I know why he is here. I've fattened him up and pampered him to the point where he is convinced that I'm a great animal lover. He worships the very ground I levitate above, the little nincompoop. But you will understand, most honored Mr. Slug . . ."

"Maggot!" said the other, rather sharply this time.

His pale countenance was illuminated solely by the nervous flickering of the fire and now looked extremely inhospitable.

The sorcerer literally wilted. "Forgive me, forgive me." He struck his forehead with the palm of his hand. "I'm a bit distraught, the stress, you know. It was pretty nerve-racking fulfilling my contract and keeping one step ahead of this spy in my own home at the same time. Even if he is a simpleton, his sight and hearing are excellent—as with all cats. I have been forced to work under the most adverse circumstances, you must admit. Above all, unfortunately, it has cost me time, a lot of time, most honored sir, ahem—"

"Distressing," interrupted Mr. Maggot, "most distressing indeed. However, all of that is really your concern, dear Minister. That doesn't change the contract any. Or could I be mistaken?"

Preposteror squirmed. "Believe me, I would have gladly vivisected that cursed cat, broiled it alive on a skewer, or kicked it all the way to the moon a long time ago, but that would have alerted the High Council of Animals for sure. They know that he is living with me. And it is much more difficult to deal with animals than with gnomes and other such riffraff—or even with people. People are hardly any trouble, but have you ever tried hypnotizing a locust or a wild boar? Nothing doing! And if all the animals on earth, large and small, were suddenly to unite and attack us, then no magic potion would save us! That's why extreme caution is required! Please explain that to His Hellish Excellency, your most honored boss."

Mr. Maggot took his briefcase from the chair and turned to the sorcerer. "Conveying explanations is not within my department."

"What do you mean?" screamed Preposteror. "His Excellency has to understand. It's in his own best interests. After all, I'm no magician. That is to say, of course I am, but there are limits—especially time limits—even for me. And what's the terrible rush, anyway? The end of the world is nigh, in any case—we're well on our way. One or two years more or less aren't going to make such a difference."

"I mean," said Mr. Maggot, responding to Preposteror's initial question with icy courtesy, "that you have been warned. At the stroke of midnight, at the turn of the year, I shall return. Those are my orders. Should you not have fulfilled your contractual quota of evil-doing by then . . ."

"What then?"

"Then, my dear Shadow Sorcery Minister," said Mr. Maggot, "you can count on a personal foreclosure *ex officio*. I wish you a merry New Year's Eve."

"Wait," cried Preposteror. "One more thing, please, Mr. Slug . . . uh . . . Mr. Maggot . . ."

But the visitor had vanished.

The sorcerer sank down in his armchair, removed his thick glasses, and covered his face with his hands. If black magicians could cry he certainly would have done so. But only a few dry kernels of salt trickled from his eyes.

"What to do?" he croaked. "By all the test tubes and tortures, what to do?"

Magic—be it good or bad—is no simple matter. Most amateurs think that all you have to do is murmur some secret hocus-pocus—at the very most it might be necessary to wave around a magic wand like a conductor—and presto, the metamorphosis or conjuring is achieved.

But that's not all there is to it. In reality, *every* kind of magic is incredibly complicated; one needs an enormous amount of knowledge, masses of paraphernalia, material that is, for the most part, very hard to obtain, as well as days, and sometimes months, of preparation. Plus the fact that it is *always* an extremely dangerous business, for even the slightest mistake can have a totally unforeseeable effect.

With flowing dressing gown, Beelzebub Preposteror

ran through the rooms and corridors of his house in desperate search of a means for his salvation. But he knew only too well that it was already too late for everything. He moaned and sighed like a wretched ghost, all the while delivering a mumbled soliloquy. His steps reverberated in the silence of the house.

He was no longer able to fulfill his contract and now cared only about saving his own skin by hiding from the hellish bailiff, somehow or somewhere.

Of course, he could turn into something else, into a rat, for example, or a common snowman—or into a field of electromagnetic oscillations (whereby he would, however, be visible as a picture disturbance on all the television screens in town), but he knew very well that he could not thus hoodwink the emissary of His Hellish Excellency, who would recognize him in every form or shape.

And it was just as pointless to escape somewhere far away, to the Sahara Desert or the North Pole or the mountaintops of Tibet, for spatial distances made no difference at all to this visitor. For a moment the sorcerer even considered hiding in the town cathedral, behind the altar or in the steeple, but he immediately dropped the idea since it seemed in no way certain to him that hellish officials have any difficulties nowadays walking in and out of churches as they please.

Preposteror rushed through the library, where ancient tomes and brand-new periodicals stood row upon row. He skimmed over the titles on the leather spines of the books, including *The Abolition of Conscience, A Manual for the Pollution of Fountains,* and *The Encyclopedic Dictionary of Curses and Spells*—but there was nothing that could be of use to him in his dire straits.

He hurried on from room to room.

The Villa Nightmare was a huge, dark box, full of little cockeyed towers, steeples, and bays on the outside and of irregularly shaped rooms, crooked corridors, rickety stairs, and cobweb-covered vaults on the inside—exactly the way you would imagine a proper haunted house to be. Preposteror himself had originally designed the plans of this house, for in matters of architecture his taste was entirely conservative. During moments of high spirits he often called the villa his "cozy little home." But at the moment he was far removed from such jest.

He was now in a long, dark corridor, the walls of which were covered with high shelves filled with hundreds and thousands of large preserving jars. This was the collection he had offered to show Mr. Maggot and which he called his "natural history museum." In each of these jars was an imprisoned elemental spirit. There were all manner of dwarfs, brownies, miniature hobgoblins, and flower elves alongside nymphs, little mermaids with colorful fish tails, tiny water sprites and sylphs, and even a few fire spirits called salamanders who had been hiding in Preposteror's chimney. All the jars were neatly labeled with a precise description of the contents, as well as the date of imprisonment.

The creatures sat motionless in their prisons, for the sorcerer had put them under continual hypnosis. He woke them up only occasionally, to carry out his cruel experiments on them.

Incidentally, among them was a particularly hideous little monster, a so-called book grump, also known in common parlance as a smartass or nitpicker. These little spirits normally spend their lives grumping about books. Research has not yet determined with any certainty why such creatures exist at all and the sorcerer himself was only keeping him in order to get to the bottom of it through lengthy observation. He had been fairly certain that the spirits could somehow be used for his purposes, but now they no longer interested him. It was only habit that prompted him, in passing, to knock here and there on a jar with his knuckles. Not a thing stirred.

Eventually he arrived at a certain small bay room, on the door of which was written:

VIRTUOSO MAURICIO DI MAURO

The little chamber was furnished with every luxury a spoiled cat could desire. There were several old pieces of upholstered furniture for sharpening one's claws, and balls of wool and other toys lay all around. On a small, low table stood a saucer with sweet cream, and several others with all kinds of appetizing tidbits; there was even a mirror at cat's-eye level, in front of which one could clean and admire oneself. And the crowning touch was a cozy little basket in the form of a small four-poster canopy bed with blue velvet cushions and curtains.

In this small bed lay a fat little tomcat, all curled up and fast asleep. Perhaps the word "fat" is not quite sufficient, for he was, in point of fact, as round as a ball. Since his fur was three-tone—rusty-brown, black, and white—he looked rather like a ridiculously spotted, overstuffed sofa pillow with four somewhat short legs and a pitiful tail.

When Mauricio had arrived here by secret order of the High Council of Animals more than a year ago, he had been ill and mangy and so emaciated that you could count his ribs one by one. At first he had pretended to the sorcerer that he was simply a stray; a very clever plan, he thought. When he noticed, however, that he not only was not chased away but instead was spoiled beyond all measure, he very quickly forgot his mission. Soon he was literally captivated by the sorcerer. Of course, Mauricio was quite easily carried away—most of all by anyone who flattered him and whose life-style fit his notion of refinement.

"We members of high society quite simply know what counts," he had frequently explained to the sorcerer. "Even in poverty we keep our standards up to par."

This was one of his favorite expressions, although he did not quite know what it actually meant.

And a few weeks later he had told the sorcerer: "You may at first have taken me for quite an ordinary stray. I do not bear you a grudge for that. How could you have suspected that, in fact, I stem from an ancient lineage of knights. There were also many famous singers in the di Mauro family. You may not believe it, since my voice is a little brittle at the moment"—indeed, it sounded more like a frog's than a cat's—"but I, too, used to be a famous minnesinger and melted the proudest of hearts with my love songs. My ancestors came from Naples, home to all truly great singers, as is well known. Our coat of arms read 'Beauty and Audacity,' and the one or the other applied to every member of my clan. But then I fell ill. Nearly all the cats in the area where I lived fell ill all of a sudden. At least those who had eaten fish. And well-bred cats just happen to prefer eating fish. But the fish was poisonous because the river whence it came was polluted. That is how I lost my wonderful voice. Almost all the others died. My whole family is now in Kitty Heaven with the Great Tom."

Preposteror had feigned great distress, although he knew only too well why the river was polluted. He had displayed the deepest compassion for Mauricio; he even called him a "tragic hero." This had pleased the little cat no end.

"If you want me to and trust me"—these had been the sorcerer's words—"I will restore you to health and give you back your voice. I will find a proper medication for you. But you will have to have patience, it will take time. And above all, you must do what I tell you. Agreed?"

Naturally Mauricio agreed. From that day on, he referred to Preposteror only as his "dear Maestro." He barely remembered the commission of the High Council of Animals.

Of course, he had no idea that, because of his black mirror and other magic means of information, Beelzebub Preposteror had long known why the cat had been sent to his home. And the Shadow Sorcery Minister had immediately decided to exploit Mauricio's small foible in order to render him harmless in a way which would not raise the cat's suspicions in the least. Indeed, the little cat felt as if he was in the land of milk and honey. He ate and slept, and slept and ate, and got fatter and more and more comfortable, and had, in the meantime, even become too lazy to catch mice.

Still, nobody can sleep for weeks and months without interruption, not even a cat. And so Mauricio had risen once in a while, after all, and roamed through the house on his stubby legs, with a paunch which by now almost touched the floor. Preposteror had to be constantly on guard lest the cat catch him at one of his evil conjurings. And this had put him in his present, desperate situation.

Now he stood before the little canopy bed and lowered his bloodthirsty gaze on the snoring ball of dappled fluff which lay upon the velvet pillows.

"Cursed son of a tomcat," he whispered, "it's all your fault."

The little cat began purring in his sleep.

"If I have to go down," Preposteror murmured, "then at least I'll have the satisfaction of wringing your neck first."

His long, knobby fingers twitched toward the neck of Mauricio, who turned on his back without waking, stretching his paws and luxuriously exposing his throat.

The sorcerer pulled back. "No," he said softly, "it won't do me any good—and besides, there will be time for that later."

A short time later, the sorcerer was back in his laboratory, writing at his desk by the glow of a lamp.

He had decided to make a will.

In a florid and hurried hand, he had already written:

My Last Will and Testament
I, Beelzebub Preposteror, Shadow Sorcery Minister, Professor, Ph.D., and so on and so forth, being of sound mind and body, and one hundred and eighty-seven years, one month, and two weeks of age on this day . . . do hereby bequeath . . .

He paused and chewed on the tip of his fountain pen, which wrote with blue cyanide instead of ink.

"Quite a ripe old age," he muttered, "but still much too young for the likes of me—much too young to go to hell, in any case."

His aunt, the witch, was almost three hundred but still extremely active professionally.

He gave a start when the little cat suddenly sprang onto the desk and yawned, daintily curling his tongue, thoroughly stretching himself front and back, and sneezing heartily a few times.

"Phooey," he meowed. "What's that terrible stench?"

He sat down right on the will and began cleaning himself.

"Has our virtuoso had a good night?" the sorcerer asked testily, shooing him aside with a less than gentle hand.

"I don't know," complained Mauricio. "I'm terribly tired all the time. I really don't know why. Have we had any company?"

"Not a soul," growled the sorcerer in an unfriendly manner, "and don't bother me now. I've got work to do and it's very urgent."

Mauricio sniffed the air. "But it smells so funny. Some stranger has been here."

"Nonsense," said Preposteror. "You're imagining things. Now be quiet."

The cat began washing his face with his paws, but suddenly he stopped and stared wide-eyed at the sorcerer. "What's the matter, dear Maestro? You look so terribly depressed."

Preposteror dismissed this with a nervous wave of his

hand. "Nothing is the matter. Now be so good as to leave me in peace, understand?"

But Mauricio did not. Quite the contrary, he sat back down on the will, rubbed his head against the sorcerer's hand, and purred softly. "I can well imagine why you're sad, Maestro. Here you are all alone, without a friend in the world, on this night, on New Year's Eve, when all the world is making merry. I feel so sorry for you."

"I'm not all the world," snarled Preposteror.

"That is true," agreed the little cat. "You're a genius and a great benefactor of both man and beast. And the truly great are always lonely. I ought to know. But would you not perhaps like to step out for just a little bit and have some fun? It would surely do you a world of good."

"A typically prepussterous idea," answered the sorcerer, who was getting more irritated by the minute. "I don't like merrymaking."

"But, Maestro," continued Mauricio eagerly, "don't they say joy shared is joy doubled?"

Preposteror brought his hand down with a bang on the table. "It has been scientifically proven," he said sharply, "that a share of something is always less than the whole. And I don't share with anybody, remember that!"

"Will do," answered the startled cat. And then added, in a flattering tone of voice, "After all, you've got me."

"Indeed," growled the sorcerer, "you're all I need."

"Truly?" asked Mauricio happily. "Am I all you need?"

Preposteror snorted impatiently. "Now be gone with you! Beat it! Go to your room! I have some thinking to do. I've got worries."

"Could I perhaps be of some help in any way, dear Maestro?" inquired the little cat assiduously.

The sorcerer moaned and rolled his eyes. "Oh, well," he sighed, "if you insist, then stir potion No. 92 in that cauldron over the fire. But take care that you don't doze off again, or who knows what will happen."

Mauricio sprang down from the table, scurried over to the fireplace on his short stubby legs, and grasped the wand of mountain crystal with his front paws.

"Must be a very important remedy," he conjectured

as he began stirring gently. "Is it perhaps the medication for my voice that you have sought so long?"

"Will you shut up now!" the sorcerer snapped at him.

"Yes, Maestro," Mauricio answered obediently.

It was quiet for a long while. The only sound was the blowing of the snowstorm around the house.

"Maestro," the little cat ventured, almost whisperingly. "Maestro, there is something I must get off my chest."

Since Preposteror did not answer, but only leaned his head on his hand with an exhausted gesture, Mauricio continued a little louder: "I must confess something to you which has been weighing on my conscience for a long time."

"Conscience." Preposteror screwed up his mouth. "What do you know, even cats have one."

"Oh, very much so," Mauricio assured him solemnly. "Perhaps not every cat, but I do for sure. I come from noble stock, after all."

The sorcerer leaned back and closed his eyes with an expression of suffering on his face.

"You see," explained Mauricio haltingly, "I am not what I appear to be."

"Who is," said Preposteror ambiguously.

The cat continued stirring. He stared into the black brew. "All the time that I've been here I've kept something from you, Maestro. And I am frightfully ashamed because of it. That is why I've decided to confess everything to you on this special evening."

The sorcerer opened his eyes and studied Mauricio through his thick glasses. His lips twitched with irony, but the little cat did not notice.

"You know better than anyone, Maestro, that bad things are happening all over the world. More and more creatures are taking ill, more and more trees are dying, and more and more bodies of water are polluted. This is why we, the animals, called a big meeting quite a while ago, a secret one, of course, and decided to find out who or what is the cause of all this misery. To this purpose our High Council dispatched secret agents everywhere who were supposed to observe what is really going on. And that is how I came to you, dear Maestro—to spy on you."

He paused and looked with big glowing eyes at the sorcerer. "Believe me," he went on, "it was very difficult for me, Maestro, for this activity does not suit my noble nature. I did it because I had to. It was my duty to the other animals."

He paused again and then added meekly, "Are you very angry with me?"

"Don't stop stirring!" said the sorcerer, who had trouble stifling a giggle, despite his gloomy mood.

"Can you forgive me, Maestro?"

"It's all right, Mauricio, I forgive you. Let's let bygones be bygones!"

"Oh," the little cat sighed, deeply moved, "what a noble heart! As soon as I've recovered and am no longer so tired, I'll drag myself to the High Council of Animals and report what a good soul you are. That is my solemn promise to you for the New Year."

These last words pitched the sorcerer into a bad mood again immediately.

"Stop with the sob stuff!" he bellowed hoarsely. "It gets on my nerves."

Mauricio kept silent, flabbergasted. He could find no explanation for his Maestro's sudden rudeness.

At that very moment there was a knock on the door.

The sorcerer sat bolt upright.

Then came a second knock, loud and clear.

Mauricio had stopped stirring and remarked dimwittedly, "Maestro, I think there was a knock at the door."

"Shush!" hissed the sorcerer. "Quiet!"

The wind shook the shutters.

"Not already!" gnashed Preposteror. "By all that stinks and sizzles, that's not fair!"

There was a third knock-knock, now quite impatient.

The sorcerer covered his ears with both hands. "I want to be left in peace. I'm not at home."

The knocking turned into hammering, and through the wind and wuthering outside one could vaguely hear a croaking voice which sounded rather angry.

"Mauricio," whispered the sorcerer, "dear kitty, would you be so kind as to open the door and say that I went on a trip unexpectedly. Simply say I went to visit my old aunt Tyrannia Vampirella and celebrate New Year's Eve with her."

"But, Maestro," said the cat in surprise, "that would be an out-and-out lie. Do you really ask that of me?"

The sorcerer rolled his eyes heavenward and groaned. "I can't very well say it myself, can I?"

"All right, Maestro, all right. I'd do anything for you."

Mauricio scurried to the front door and, summoning all his waning strength, pushed a stool under the door handle, climbed up, and turned the gigantic key until the lock opened, all the while hanging on to the handle. A gust of wind tore open the door and raged through the rooms, so that the papers swirled about in the laboratory and the green flames in the fireplace lay back horizontally.

But no one was there.

The cat took a few cautious steps outside the door, peered to all sides in the darkness, came back in, and shook the snow from his fur.

"Nothing," he said. "It must have been a mistake. But where are you, Maestro?"

Preposteror appeared from behind the armchair. "No one is there? Really?" he asked.

"Definitely not," Mauricio confirmed.

The sorcerer rushed out into the hallway, slammed the front door shut, and locked it several times. Then he came back in, threw himself in his chair, and lamented, "They can't wait. They want to drive me insane already."

"Who?" asked Mauricio in surprise.

There was another knock, and this time it sounded furious.

Preposteror's face was distorted in a grimace expressing fear and loathing at the same time. It was not a pretty sight.

"Not with me!" he gasped. "Oh no, not with me! We'll see about that."

He pussyfooted out into the hallway, with the little cat pussyfooting eagerly in tow.

On his left hand the sorcerer wore a ring sporting a large ruby. Naturally this was a magic stone; it could swallow and store enormous quantitites of light. When properly loaded, it was a devastating weapon.

Preposteror slowly lifted his hand, shut one eye, aimed—and a threadlike red laser beam sizzled through the corridor, leaving a smoking pinprick of a mark in the massive front door. The sorcerer fired a second shot and a third, and again and again, until the massive wooden planks looked like a sieve and the ruby's energy had been exhausted.

"Well, that should do it," he said, and took a deep breath. "Peace and quiet at last."

He went back to the laboratory and sat down at his desk to continue writing.

"But, Maestro," stammered the little cat in horror, "what if you hit someone out there . . . ?"

"It would serve them right," growled Preposteror. "What are they sneaking around in front of my house for?"

"But you have no idea who it was! Perhaps it was one of your friends."

"I have no friends."

"Or someone who needs your help."

The sorcerer uttered a short, mirthless laugh. "You don't know life, my little one. He who shoots first shoots best. Remember that."

At which point there was another knock at the door.

Preposteror just sat there grinding his jaws.

"The window!" cried Mauricio. "I think it is at the window, Maestro."

He sprang onto the sill, opened the window, and peeked out through a slit in the shutter.

"There's someone sitting there," he whispered. "It looks like a bird, a kind of raven, I think."

Preposteror still did not speak. He merely raised his hands defensively.

"Perhaps it's an emergency," suggested the little cat.

And without waiting for an order from the sorcerer, he pushed open the shutter.

Accompanied by a cloud of snow there fluttered into the laboratory a bird so ragged that it looked a lot like a large, shapeless potato stuck haphazardly with a few feathers here and there.

It landed in the middle of the floor, slid a ways on its skinny legs before coming to a standstill, fluffed up its skimpy feathers, and opened its substantial beak wide.

"Well! Well! Well!" it croaked at an impressive volume. "You sure take your time letting someone in. A creature could catch its death out there. And you get shot at to boot. There, you see—my last tail feather has had it. What kind of manners is that? Have we become barbarians?"

Suddenly he realized that there was a cat staring at him with great glowing eyes. He tucked his head between his feathers, which made him look kind of hunchbacked, and managed no more than a feeble croak: "Uh-oh, a bird-eater! That's just what I needed. Thanks a lot. This will come to no good end."

Mauricio, who had never in his short life caught a single bird—and certainly not such a big, scary one—did not have the faintest idea at first that the bird was referring to him.

"Hello!" he meowed with dignity. "Welcome, stranger."

The sorcerer was still staring silently and suspiciously at the odd feathered creature.

The raven felt increasingly uncomfortable. He gazed with tilted head back and forth between the cat and the sorcerer and at last rasped, "If you gentlemen don't mind, I suggest somebody shut the window, because there's nobody coming after behind me but it's pretty durned drafty and I've got rawmatism, or whatever you call it, in my left wing anyway."

The cat closed the window, sprang down from the sill, and started circling stealthily around the intruder. He only wanted to see whether the raven was all right. But the latter seemed to misinterpret Mauricio's concern.

Meanwhile, Preposteror had regained his power of speech.

"Mauricio," he commanded, "ask this jailbird who he is and what he wants of us."

"My good Maestro wishes to inquire as to your appellation and the purpose of your visit," said the cat in a distinguished purr, circling closer all the while.

The bird turned his head to follow the cat, never letting Mauricio out of his sight.

37

"My best greetings to your Maestro"—he desperately winked at the cat with one eye—"and my worthy name is Jacob Scribble, if you please, and I am, so to speak, the airy errand boy of Madam Tyrannia Vampirella, his honored aunt"—now winking with the other eye—"and apart from that, I am definitely not no jailbird, if you please, but an old raven to whom life has put many a hard test; you might well say a sad sack of feathers, you might say."

"Well, what do you know, a raven!" sneered Preposteror. "Of course, you have to say so, or no one's going to guess."

"Ha ha, very funny," rasped Jacob Scribble to himself in a subdued voice.

"Sad sack?" inquired Mauricio sympathetically. "What manner of sadness do you mean? Speak without fear, my good Maestro will help you."

"I mean the bad luck what I always have," Jacob explained gloomily. "For example, now I've got to run into a killer bird-eater, of all things, and I lost my feathers back when I strayed into a poison cloud. There's more and more of them lately; nobody knows why." He winked at the cat again. "And you can tell your good Maestro from me that he doesn't need to look at me if my ragged wardrobe bothers him. I don't have nothing better anymore."

Mauricio looked up at Preposteror. "You see, Maestro, it was an emergency, after all."

"Why don't you ask this raven why he keeps winking at you secretly?" said the sorcerer.

Jacob Scribble was quicker than the cat. "That is involuntary, Sorcery Minister, it doesn't mean a thing. It's just my nerves."

"Is that so," drawled Preposteror, "and why might we be so nervous?"

"Because I've got something against such bumptious guys who talk so fancy and have such sharp claws and two taillights in their face like him."

It finally dawned on Mauricio that he had just been insulted. Naturally he couldn't sit still for that. He drew himself up to as impressive a stature as he could, bristled, laid his ears back, and spat, "Maestro, would you allow me to pluck this impudent blabberbeak?"

The sorcerer took the cat on his lap and petted him. "Not yet, my little hero. Calm down. After all, he says he was sent by my most highly esteemed aunt. Let's hear what he has to say. I only wonder whether one can believe a word he says. What do you think?"

"He certainly has no manners," purred Mauricio. The raven's wings drooped and he said, "Oh, peck my tailfeathers, the both of you!"

"It is surprising," said Preposteror, while he continued stroking the cat's fur, "it is truly surprising what common help my heretofore so distinguished auntie has taken to surrounding herself with."

"What?!" screeched the raven. "Now, that pops my cork! Who's common here? It's not no fun when someone in my condition flaps through night and storm to announce his boss and he arrives just in time for supper, not the kind where he gets something between his beak, but where he's on the menu himself. I'd like to ask out loud just who is common here."

"What are you saying, Raven?" asked Preposteror in alarm. "Aunt Tyrannia is coming here? When?"

Jacob Scribble was still livid and hopping around on the floor. "Now! At once! Right away! In the blink of an eye! Any second! She's almost here!"

Preposteror sank back in his armchair and moaned, "Oh, warts! That's all I needed!"

The raven observed him with tilted head and rasped contentedly, "Aha, sad news, so it seems. That's typical for me."

"I haven't seen Aunt Tye face to face for half a century," the sorcerer whined. "What does she want here all of a sudden? Today of all days is a very bad day."

The raven shrugged his wings. "She says she absolutely must come today and spend New Year's Eve with her beloved nephew, she says, because her nephew, so she says, has some kind of a special recipe for some kind of punch, she says, what she herself desperately needs, she said."

Preposteror shoved the cat off his lap and jumped up. "She knows everything," he exclaimed. "She only wants to take advantage of my situation, by all the devil's tumors. She wants to get on my good side under the pretext of family ties, only to perpetrate intellectual thievery. I know her, you bet I know her!"

Then he uttered an interminable Babylonian or ancient Egyptian curse, at which point all the glass receptacles in the room started humming and clinking and a dozen balls of lightning hissed in a zigzag across the floor.

Mauricio, who had never experienced this side of his Maestro, was so frightened that he fled with an enormous leap onto the head of a stuffed shark, which hung on the wall among other stuffed trophies.

There he discovered, to his renewed horror, that the raven had done the same and that they were holding each other tight without noticing it. They immediately let go in embarrassment.

The Shadow Sorcery Minister searched among the mountains of paper on his desk with trembling hands, got everything mixed up, and bellowed, "By all the acid rains, she shall not see so much as a decimal point of my precious equations! That insidious hyena seems to think she can get all the results of my research *for free* now. But she's barking up the wrong tree! She's not going to inherit a thing, not a thing! I'm going to store the files with the most important formulas in my secret super-sorcery-proof cellar without any further ado. She'll never get in there. Neither she nor anyone else."

He was about to run off, but stopped in his tracks and searched the laboratory with wild eyes. "Mauricio, holy pesticide, where are you?"

"Here I am, Maestro," answered Mauricio from up on the shark's head.

"Listen," the sorcerer called up to him, "you keep an eye on that son of a raven while I'm gone, understand!

But don't go to sleep again. Watch out that he doesn't stick his beak into things that are none of his business. It would be best if you took him to your chamber and guarded the door. By no means trust him, and don't get drawn in by any conversation or attempts at familiarity. I'm holding you responsible."

He hastened away with his bilious green dressing gown fluttering behind.

The two animals sat facing each other.

The raven stared at the cat and the cat stared at the raven.

"Well?" asked Jacob after a while.

"Well what?" spat Mauricio.

The raven winked once again. "You still don't know what's going on, comrade?"

Mauricio was confused, but on no account did he want to show it, which is why he said, "Shut your big beak! My Maestro said no talking."

"But he's gone now," croaked Jacob, "and we can speak openly, comrade."

"No attempts at familiarity!" retorted Mauricio sternly. "Save yourself the trouble. You are brazen and common and I don't like you."

"Nobody likes me anyway, so I'm used to it," answered Jacob. "But the two of us still have to work together now. That's our mission, after all."

"Be quiet!" growled the little cat from deep in his throat, trying to look as dangerous as possible. "We're going to my room now. Jump down—and don't you try to escape! March!"

Jacob Scribble looked at Mauricio and shook his head in disbelief. "Are you really that stupid or are you just pretending?"

Mauricio didn't know how to react. Ever since he had been alone with Jacob, the raven had suddenly seemed much bigger and his beak much sharper and more dangerous. Mauricio arched his back involuntarily and his whiskers bristled. Poor Jacob's heart skipped a beat, as he took this to be a serious threat. He fluttered obediently down to the floor. The little cat, who was himself quite taken aback by his effect on the raven, followed.

"Let me be and I'll let you be," Jacob clucked and ducked.

Mauricio felt grand. "Forward march, stranger!" he commanded.

"Well, that's the way the cookie crumbles," croaked Jacob in defeat. "I wish I had stayed in the nest with Clara."

"Who is Clara?"

"Just my poor wife," said Jacob.

And he stalked off on his skinny legs, with the cat close behind.

When they reached the long, dark corridor with its many jars, Mauricio, who had done some thinking, asked, "Why do you keep calling me comrade, anyway?"

"Holy hangman!—because that's what we are," answered Jacob, "or at least we used to be, I thought."

"A cat and a bird can never be comrades," declared Mauricio proudly. "Don't put on airs, raven. Cats and birds are natural enemies."

"Naturally," confirmed Jacob. "I mean, naturally that would be only natural. But naturally only when the situation is natural. Natural enemies are sometimes comrades in unnatural situations."

"Slow down!" said Mauricio. "I don't understand. Express yourself more clearly."

Jacob stopped and turned around. "You also came here as a secret agent to observe your Maestro, or didn't you?"

"What do you mean?" asked Mauricio, now totally confused. "You, too? But why has the High Council sent yet another agent here?"

"No, not here," said Jacob. "I mean, not me. I mean, you get me all confizzled in the head with your slow-pokey brain. Now listen: I spy on my Madam Witch, same as you spy on your Monsewer Sorcerer. Have you finally swallowed the worm?"

Mauricio sat down in astonishment. "Is that honestly so?"

"As honest as I am a sad sack of a raven," sighed Jacob. "By the way, would you mind if I scratched myself? I've had this itch ever since I got here."

"But I beg of you!" responded Mauricio with a magnanimous wave of his paw. "After all, we are comrades."

He wound his tail elegantly around himself and watched while Jacob scratched his head thoroughly with one claw.

All of a sudden Mauricio felt a deep affection for the old raven. "Why didn't you identify yourself right from the beginning?"

"I did," croaked Jacob. "I kept winking at you the whole time."

"Aha!" cried Mauricio. "But couldn't you have come right out and said it?"

Now it was Jacob's turn to be confounded. "Said it?"

he cawed. "So that your boss could hear everything? You're a riot."

"My Maestro knows everything, anyway."

"What?" snapped the raven. "Did he find out?"

"No," said Mauricio. "I let him in on it."

The raven's beak hung open in disbelief.

"You've got to be kidding," he exclaimed finally. "That knocks me right off my branch! Say that again!"

"I just had to," Mauricio explained with a self-important mien. "It would not have been chivalrous to deceive him any longer. I have observed and tested him for a long time and have come to the conclusion that he is a noble human being and a true genius and worthy of our confidence. Although he is acting a little odd today, I must admit. In any case, he has treated me like a prince the whole time. And that shows what a kindly man and benefactor of all animals he is."

Jacob stared at Mauricio in consternation. "I don't believe it! How can just one cat be so stupid? Maybe two or three together, but just one? Now you've blown it, my boy, now you've blown everything; now the whole plan of the animals is bound to fail, to fail miserably, in fact. I saw it coming, I saw it coming from the very start!"

"But you don't know my Maestro at all," meowed the insulted cat. "He's usually a totally different person."

"To you, maybe!" screeched Jacob. "He's got you all buttered up—and fattened up as well, as anyone can see."

"Who do you think you are?" spat Mauricio, now properly miffed. "How come you know everything better than I?"

"Don't you have eyes in your head?" screamed Jacob. "Just take a look around here! What do you think *all that* is, anyway?"

With outstretched wing, he pointed at the shelves full of innumerable jars.

"That? That is an infirmary," said Mauricio. "The Maestro himself told me so. He is trying to heal the poor gnomes and elves. What do you know about it, anyway!"

"What do I know?" Jacob Scribble was getting more and more beside himself. "Shall I tell you what that is? A prison, that's what that is! A torture chamber is what that is! In reality your wonderful Maestro is one of the very worst people there are in this whole world, that's what he is! And that's a fact, you nincompoop! Ha ha —a goody-goody! A benefactor! Don't make me laugh! You know what he can do? Pollute the air, that's what. Poison the water, make man and beast ill, destroy fields and forests—that's what your Maestro is really good at, and nothing else!"

Mauricio choked with outrage. "You . . . you . . . you take that back, you slanderer, or else . . . or else . . ."

His fur bristled so, he looked twice as fat as he already was. "I shall not allow you to insult this great man. Apologize, or I'll teach you what respect is, you jailbird!"

But there was no stopping Jacob now that he was warmed up. "Just you try!" he screeched. "You fat milquetoast, you flabby couch potato! The only thing you're good for is playing with balls of yarn and sprawling out on the sofa! Beat it, you saucer licker! Or else I'll wrap you up in a package and send you back home to your cute little kitty-cat clan!"

Mauricio's eyes started to glow like hot coals. "I stem from an ancient lineage of Neapolitan knights. My ancestors go all the way back to King Oedipuss. I won't stand for my family being insulted! And certainly not by some fly-by-night scoundrel like you!"

"Ha ha!" screeched Jacob. "Then your ancestors used up all the brains in the family for themselves and didn't leave any for you."

Mauricio whipped out his claws. "Do you have any idea whom you are talking to, you miserable molting dervish? You are in the presence of a great artist. I am a famous minnesinger and melted the proudest of hearts before I lost my voice."

The old raven burst out with an impertinent laugh. "I can believe that you're a mini-singer with your mini-stature and your mini-brain. Just don't get so uppity, you puffed-up bottle brush!"

"Illiterate lowbrow," spat Mauricio with profound disdain. "You don't even know what a minnesinger is. And your language comes right out of the gutter, you miserable vagabond!"

"I don't give a hoot," Jacob screamed back. "I've got

freedom of beak, because I've got one after all, but you don't, you crummy cat baron . . ."

And all of a sudden, before either of them really knew how it had come about and who had started it, they were a bundle of feathers and fur rolling around on the floor. They scuffled about and the sparks flew. The cat bit and scratched and the raven pecked and pinched. But since they were both pretty much the same size and strength, neither could gain the upper hand. Sometimes one of them fled and was chased by the other, and sometimes the other way around. Without noticing it, they had fought their way back into the laboratory. Jacob had sunk his beak into Mauricio's tail and this hurt the

little cat horribly, while, at the same time, Mauricio had the raven in a headlock so that he was slowly suffocating.

"Give up," groaned Mauricio, "or else you are a dead duck!"

"You give up first," coughed Jacob, "or else I'll snip your tail off!"

And then both let go at the same time and sat facing each other, all out of breath.

With tears in his eyes the little cat tried to straighten out his tail, which no longer looked elegant in the least but had been bent into a zigzag, while the melancholy raven eyed the feathers scattered on the floor, feathers he really couldn't spare.

Yet, as is often the case after such skirmishes, the two of them felt relatively peaceable and ready to make up. Jacob was thinking that he shouldn't have been quite so rough with the fat little cat, and Mauricio was wondering if he hadn't perhaps done the poor, unfortunate raven quite an injustice.

"Please forgive me," he meowed.

"I'm sorry, too," croaked Jacob.

"You know," Mauricio said after a while in a trembling voice, "I simply can't believe what you said before. How can someone treat a great cat artist like myself so well and be a nasty villain at the same time? It's not possible."

"I'm afraid it is," said Jacob, and nodded bitterly. "I'm afraid it is. He didn't treat you well at all. He only *tamed* you in order to pull the wool over your eyes. My boss,

Madam Tyrannia, tried to do the same with me. But I didn't let myself be tamed. I only faked it. But she didn't notice. I pulled the wool over *her* eyes."

He laughed cunningly. "In any case, I managed to find out a lot about her—and about your fine Maestro as well. What's keeping him so long, anyhow?"

They both listened, but there was nothing to hear. Only the sound of the stormy wind whimpering and whistling outside the house.

In order to reach his absolutely sorcery-proof secret cellar, Preposteror had to go through a veritable labyrinth of subterranean passageways, each of which was magically sealed off by several doors, which could be opened and closed only in an ever so complicated manner. It was a time-consuming procedure.

Jacob slid closer to Mauricio and whispered in a conspiratorial voice, "Now listen up, kitty. My madam is not only your Maestro's aunt, she also pays his salary. He supplies her with whatever she wants, and she makes big deals with all that poison stuff he brews. She's a money witch, you understand?"

"No," said Mauricio. "What is a money witch?"

"I don't know exactly what it is myself," Jacob admitted. "She does magic with money. Somehow she gets it to multiply on its own. Each of them is already bad enough, but when money witches and laboratory sorcerers get together—good night!—then things get really gloomy in this world."

Mauricio felt terribly tired all of a sudden. This was all simply too much for him and he longed for his velvet cushions.

"If you're already so well informed," he said with a bit of a whine, "why haven't you long since gone to our High Council and reported it?"

"I was counting on you," answered Jacob Scribble gloomily, "because I have no proof up to now that the two of them are in cahoots with each other. I can tell you, as far as human beings are concerned, it's money that makes the world go round. Especially for the likes of your Maestro and my madam. They'll do anything for money, and with money they can do anything. It's their nastiest magic spell, it is. That's why we animals didn't get wise to them up to now, because we have nothing like it. All I knew was that one of our agents was spying on Preposteror as well—I just didn't know who. Well, I thought to myself, together with this comrade we'll finally get the proof we need. Especially this evening."

"Why especially this evening?" Mauricio inquired.

Without any warning the raven let loose a long, portentous croak, which echoed through all the rooms and chilled the little cat to the marrow.

"Excuse me," Jacob said, quiet once again, "that's just the way we are when something's brewing somewhere. Because we can feel it ahead of time, you see? I don't know what they're up to yet, but I'll bet my last feathers that it's outrageously humanish."

"What?"

"Well, you can't say swinish, can you, because swines don't hurt anyone. That's why I made a special flight here through night and storm. My madam doesn't know anything about it. I was counting on you. But you've clued your Maestro in, so now we can forget about everything. I really wish I had stayed in my warm nest with Amalia."

"I thought your wife's name was Clara?"

"That's a different one," Jacob croaked indignantly. "Besides, we're not discussing my wife's name but the fact that you've made a mess of everything."

Mauricio gazed at the raven in confusion. "You always seem to see the dark side of things wherever you look. You are a pessimist."

"Correct!" said Jacob Scribble dryly. "And that's why I'm almost always right. Wanna bet?"

The little cat put on a sulky face. "All right. What?"

"If *you're* right, I'll swallow a rusty nail; if *I'm* right, you'll do the same. Agreed?"

Mauricio tried hard to appear as cool as possible. Still, his voice trembled a little as he answered, "You're on! It's a bet."

Jacob Scribble nodded and immediately began inspecting the laboratory. Mauricio ran along beside him. "Are you looking for the nail already?"

"No," said the raven, "for a suitable hiding place for us."

"What for?"

"Because we have to eavesdrop on our hosts."

The little cat stopped in his tracks and said indignantly, "No, I will do no such thing. It is beneath me."

"Where?" asked Jacob.

"I mean, it is quite simply not chivalrous. It is not done. After all, I'm not a rogue!"

"But I am," quoth the raven.

"But one doesn't eavesdrop," explained Mauricio. "It just isn't done!"

"Well then, what would you do?"

"I?" Mauricio thought it over. "I would simply ask the Maestro straight out, face to face."

The raven gave the cat a sideways glance and croaked, "Very sound, Count! Face to face—I can just see his face."

Meanwhile, they had arrived in a dark corner in front of a large metal barrel with an open lid. It was labeled TOXIC WASTE.

The two animals eyed the writing.

"Can you read?" asked Jacob.

"Can't you?" said Mauricio with a slightly condescending air.

"I never learned," admitted the raven. "What does it say?"

Mauricio couldn't resist the temptation to show off in front of the raven. "It says GARBAGE, or . . . no . . . it says FUEL . . . although that looks like a z at the beginning . . ."

At that very moment a sound like the howling of a siren could be heard coming closer through the wuthering winds outside.

"That's my madam," whispered Jacob. "She always makes such a hellish racket because she likes to make a big entrance. Quick, let's hide in the barrel!"

He fluttered onto the rim, but the cat hesitated.

Now a shrill voice could be heard ringing out of the fireplace:

"Ring ring! Knock knock!
You've got a visit.

The door you unlock
And look, who is it?"

At the same time, a gust of wind howled down the chimney, flattening out the flames of the green fire and sending thick clouds of smoke billowing into the room.

"Oh my!" coughed Jacob Scribble. "She's here already. Quick, kitty, hurry up!"

The voice from the fireplace came closer and closer. It sounded as if someone was screeching through a long pipe.

"Profit makers,
Give evil thanks
To movers and shakers
In piggy banks!"

Then suddenly a grunt could be heard from the chimney and the voice mumbled, "Wait a minute . . . I think . . . I'm stuck . . . hang on . . . okay . . . yes, here we go."

The raven hopped about on the rim of the barrel and croaked, "Come on, will you! Move it! Jump!"

The little cat jumped up and the raven pushed him in with his beak, following close behind. With all their might they managed to close the lid at the last second.

The shrill voice from the fireplace was very close now.

"Can the world be bought?
Why not? Why not?
Can the world be sold?
If you've got enough gold!
Well, here's the dough,
So don't be slow!
Let's quit the rapping . . ."

Now a veritable hailstorm of coins clattered down the chimney; then there was a hefty plop in the fireplace, the cauldron of potion No. 92 tipped over, its contents sizzling away in the embers (Mr. Pick-Me-Up's Diet would not be going on sale for the time being), and, in the midst of the flaring flames, sat Tyrannia Vampirella, who squeaked,

"Why aren't you clapping?"

When they think of a witch, most people picture a haggard, wrinkly old woman with a big hump on her back, a string of hairy warts on her face, and one long, solitary

tooth in her mouth. But nowadays witches usually look completely different. In any case, Tyrannia Vampirella looked just the opposite of all that. Admittedly, she was relatively short, at least compared with Preposteror's tall frame. But she was incredibly fat. She was literally as wide as she was tall.

Her wardrobe consisted of a sulphurous-yellow evening gown with a good deal of black stripes, which made her look like an oversized hornet (sulphurous yellow being *her* favorite color).

She was dripping with gems and jewelry; even her teeth were made of solid gold, with sparkling diamond fillings. Each and every one of her chubby little sausage fingers was adorned with a ring, and even her long fingernails were gold-plated. On her head was a hat the size of a car tire, the brim of which jingled with hundreds of coins.

When she crawled out of the fireplace and stood up, she looked like a floor lamp of some kind—a very expensive one, of course.

In contrast to the witches of former times, she was immune to fire; it didn't faze her in the least. She merely slapped out the little flames still flickering on her evening gown with mild annoyance.

Her pug face, with its wobbly hanging cheeks and shopping bags under the eyes, was so heavily made up that it looked like a window display in a beauty parlor. In place of a pocketbook she carried a little safe with a combination lock under her arm.

"Hellohoho!" she called, attempting to make her shrill voice sound sweet, while peering all around. "Is anybody ho-home? Yoo hoo! Bubby!"

No reply.

Now, Tyrannia Vampirella hated it if no one paid any attention to her. Above all, her impressive entrances were extremely important to her. The fact that Preposteror had not been present at her spectacle already made her furious at him.

She instantly began snooping around among the papers on the table, but she didn't get very far, since she heard footsteps approaching. It was Preposteror, who was finally returning. She hastened toward her nephew with outstretched arms.

"Beelzebub!" she twittered. "Beelzebubby! Let me have a look at you! Is it really you?"

"It is I, Auntie Tye, it is I," he said, contorting his face in bitter creases of joy.

Tyrannia tried to hug him, which she managed only with difficulty on account of her impressive girth.

"It's you, my oh so *precious* nephew," she crowed. "By the way, I knew it was you from the start. Who else could you have been?" She giggled so hard that all the coins jingled and jangled.

Preposteror tried to escape her all-encompassing embrace and grumbled, "I also knew that it was you from the start, Auntie."

She stood on tiptoe in order to pinch his cheek. "I hope you're pleasantly surprised. Or were you maybe expecting a visit from some other cute little witch?"

"Not at all, Tye," Preposteror protested peevishly. "You know me. My work leaves me no time for such things."

"You bet I know you, Bubby," she countered impishly, "and better than anybody else. Wasn't I the one who brought you up and paid for your education? And as far as I can tell, you're still living high on the hog—at my expense."

Preposteror did not seem to enjoy being reminded of this. He answered grumpily, "And vice versa, by the looks of you."

Tyrannia released him from her embrace, took a step back, and asked menacingly, "What are you trying to say?"

"Oh, nothing," he said evasively. "You haven't changed a bit in the half century since we last saw one another, dearest Auntie."

"You, on the other hand, have aged terribly, my poor boy," she said.

"Is that so?" he countered. "In that case, I must tell you that you've grown incredibly fat, old girl."

They stared angrily at one another for a second; then Preposteror said in a conciliatory tone of voice, "Anyway, it's nice that the two of us haven't changed where it counts."

"You bet." Tyrannia nodded. "We're still just as much of one mind as we ever were."

The animals were squeezed so close together in the barrel that they could hear each other's heart beating. They scarcely dared to breathe.

The inane discussion between sorcerer and witch continued for a while. It was apparent that they were feeling each other out and that neither one trusted the other. But eventually their supply of small talk was exhausted.

In the meantime, both had taken seats opposite one another and were staring at each other through slitted eyes, like two poker players before a big hand. A frosty silence filled the room. A thick icicle formed between them in the air at the point where their gazes met, and fell with a clink to the floor.

"Now let's get down to business," said Tyrannia.

Preposteror's expression remained inscrutable. "I figured you didn't just come to share a New Year's punch with me."

The witch sat up straight in her seat. "Where the devil did you get such an idea?"

"From your raven—Jacob Scribble, or whatever his name is."

"He was here?"

"Yes, you sent him, didn't you?"

"I did *not*," said Tyrannia angrily. "I wanted my visit to be a surprise."

Preposteror smiled joylessly. "Don't take it so hard, dear Auntie Tye. At least I was able to prepare for your sweet visit."

"That raven is getting too big for his britches," the witch went on.

"My opinion exactly," Preposteror replied. "He is impertinent to a noticeable degree."

His aunt nodded. "I've had him for about a year and he's had a rebellious personality from the start."

The sorcerer and the witch found themselves staring at each other in silence once again.

Finally Preposteror asked, "How much does he know about you—and your business—anyway?"

"Not a thing," said Tyrannia. "He's nothing but a working-class stiff."

"Are you quite sure?"

"You bet!"

Jacob chuckled silently to himself and whispered in the little cat's ear, "That's what *she* thinks."

"Why do you keep the impertinent fowl in the first place?" Preposteror asked.

"Because *I* know too much about *him*."

"And what do you know about him?"

The witch's diamond fillings sparkled. "Everything."

"What does that mean?"

"He is actually a spy sent to my house to snoop on me by the High Council of Animals. That jailbird thinks he's pretty clever. He honestly believes to this day that I haven't noticed anything."

Jacob's beak fell shut with an almost audible snap. Mauricio nudged him and whispurred, "That's what *she* thinks, comrade."

The sorcerer raised his eyebrows and nodded pensively.

"Well, well, well," he said. "I, too, have had a spy in the house for some time—a complete simpleton of a cat who imagines himself to be a singer. He is gullible, gluttonous, and vain; in other words, a very pleasant companion—at least for me. It was child's play rendering him harmless from the very beginning. I've stuffed him full of food—and tranquillizers. He dozes away his days, but he's happy and contented, the little fool. He worships the very ground I walk on."

"And he doesn't suspect a thing?"

"He trusts me from the bottom of his heart," Preposteror replied. "Do you know what he did today? He confessed everything of his own free will—why he is here and who sent him. He even begged my forgiveness for betraying me all this time. Have you ever heard of anyone so stupid?"

The tension between the sorcerer and the witch gave way to an explosion of ringing laughter. It may have been a duet—but it certainly wasn't in harmony.

In the barrel, Mauricio could not suppress a tiny, silent sob. Jacob, who was just about to make a snide remark, sensed this and tactfully chose to remain silent.

"Nonetheless, extreme caution is required, my boy!" said Tyrannia, who had suddenly become serious again. "If they sneak spies into our homes, it means that the High Council of Animals has grown suspicious of us. I only wonder whose fault it is, Bubby?"

Preposteror braved his aunt's gaze and said, "You're asking me? Maybe *you* were a little too careless, Tye. Who knows how a raven brain works. Let's hope the guy doesn't ruin my stupid cat and end up putting dangerous ideas into his head."

Tyrannia looked around the laboratory. "We should cross-examine the two of them. Where are they, anyway?"

"In the cat's chamber," said the sorcerer. "I assigned Mauricio to lock the raven in and guard him there."

"And will he carry out his orders?"

"You can bet your broom on it."

"Well then, let's leave it at that for the time being," the witch decided. "We can always deal with the two of them later. I've got something more pressing to discuss with you at the moment."

Preposteror's suspicions were back in an instant. "And what might that be, Auntie?"

"You still haven't asked me *why* I came to see you."

"Well, I'm asking you now."

The witch leaned back and gazed severely at her nephew for some time. He knew that he was about to get one of her so-called curtain lectures, which he hated because they always had a hidden purpose. He drummed nervously with his fingers on the arm of his chair, looked up at the ceiling, and whistled distractedly.

"Now you listen to me, Beelzebub Preposteror," she began. "Everything you are today, you basically owe to me. Are you aware of that? Back then, when your dear parents—my brother-in-law Asmodeus and my beautiful sister Lilith—so tragically and inadvertently lost their lives during the great shipwreck they themselves had caused, I took you in and raised you. You wanted for nothing. I beat your first lessons in cruelty to animals for fun and profit into you with my own two hands, when you were still a babe in arms. Later I enrolled you in the most devilish of schools, Sodom and Gomorrah High and Ahriman College. But you were always a problem child, Bubby; I had to cover up for your peccadillos and deficiencies even when you were still a young student at the Magic Institute of Technology in Hexachusetts. After all, we are the last two remaining members of our family. All that cost me a pretty penny, as you well know. You also got your good grades in Advanced Diabolics thanks to me, because I used my influence as chairwoman of the board of Wickednickel International, Inc. I saw to it that you were accepted into the Academy of Black Arts and I introduced you to the Deepest Circles, where you made the personal acquaintance of your benefactor and namesake. All in all, I should think that you are enough in my debt so as not to refuse me a small favor, which won't cost you a thing."

Preposteror's face had assumed a pinched expression. Whenever she talked like this, she usually wanted to set him up in some way.

"It won't cost me a thing?" he drawled. "I can't wait to hear this."

"Well," said the witch, "it's hardly worth mentioning. If I'm not mistaken, there was an ancient scroll of parchment, approximately two and a half yards long, among the heirlooms left to you by your grandfather Belial Preposteror."

Preposteror nodded cautiously. "It's somewhere up in the attic. I'd have to look for it first. I packed it away because it is completely useless. Apparently it used to be much longer, but good old Grandpa Belial tore it in two during one of his famous tantrums. To me he bequeathed only the second half, wicked old man that he was. Nobody knows where the other half is. It's probably some sort of formula—unfortunately, it's completely worthless, even for you, Auntie."

"That's just it!" said Tyrannia, and smiled as if her teeth were made of rock candy. "And since I may assume that you set great store by my financial aid, now and in the future, I don't see why you couldn't make me a present of that worthless piece of parchment scroll."

His aunt's sudden interest in this heirloom made the sorcerer suspicious.

"A present?!" He spat out the word like a piece of gristle. "I never give presents. Who ever gives me any?"

Tyrannia sighed. "Well, I expected as much. Wait a minute."

She began working the combination lock of her pocketbook-safe with her golden fingernails, all the while murmuring in a businesslike tone of voice:

"Mammon, Lord of all that's pricey,
Crispy bills and clinking crowns,

Show us what makes life so spicy,
Money makes the world go round!"

Then she yanked open the tiny door of the safe and withdrew several fat rolls of bank notes, which she peeled off one at a time in front of Preposteror.

"There!" she said. "Maybe that will convince you that, once again, I've got only your profit in mind. One thousand—two thousand—three—four—how much do you want?"

Preposteror grinned like Yorick's skull. Now his old auntie had made a crucial mistake. He knew on the one hand that she had the power to produce as much money as she wanted—a black-magic specialty not at his own disposal, for he was in another field—but on the other hand, he also knew that she was the epitome of miserliness and still had the first dollar she ever produced. If she was offering such a large sum, then the half scroll of parchment had to be worth *very much* to her.

"My dearest Auntie Tye," he said, seemingly imperturbed, "I cannot help but entertain the notion that you are keeping something from me. That is not very good of you."

"I won't stand for it!" the witch replied indignantly. "That's no way for us to do business."

She got up, walked over to the fireplace, and pretended to look sulkily into the flames.

"Hey, kit-kat," Jacob whispered close to his fellow sufferer's ear, "don't go to sleep now of all times!"

Mauricio awoke with a start. "I beg your pardon," he breathed, "that comes from the tranquillizers . . . Would you please be so kind as to give me a hearty pinch?"

Jacob did so.

"Heartier still!" said Mauricio.

Jacob pinched him so hard that the little cat came within a hair of meowing out loud, but he heroically refrained.

"Thank you," he whispered with tears in his eyes. "Now I'm all right again."

"You know, Beelzebub," the witch began in a senti-mental tone of voice, "evenings like this always make me think of the good old days, when we were still all together: Uncle Cerberus and his charming wife, Me-dusa; little Nero and his sister Ghoulia; and then of course my cousin Virus, who was always a-courting me; your parents and Grandpa Belial, who let you ride bareback on his knees. Do you remember the time we had a picnic and burned down the entire forest? It was so idyllic."

"What are you getting at?" Preposteror asked mo-rosely.

"I would like to buy that scroll from you, Bubby, simply as a small remembrance of Grandfather Belial. Where's your family spirit?"

"Now you're getting silly, Auntie Tye," he an-swered.

"All right," she said, in her normal tone of voice, and

went back to her pocketbook-safe. "So, how much do you want? I'll throw in another five thousand."

She pulled out several more bankrolls and threw them at the sorcerer's feet, furious by now. Quite a respectable pile had accumulated in the meantime, in any case much more than could have fit into the small pocketbook-safe.

"Well?" she asked expectantly. "Ten thousand—my final offer! Take it or leave it."

The furrows in Preposteror's brow deepened. He stared at all that money through his thick glasses. His hands twitched, but he kept his composure. Money couldn't help him out of his desperate situation, anyway. But the more she offered him, the more certain he was that she was not offering enough. He absolutely had to find out what she had up her sleeve.

He tried to catch her off guard and took a shot in the dark, so to speak.

"Come, come, old girl," he said as calmly as he could, "of course I know that *you* have the other half of the scroll."

His aunt's face turned colors beneath her several layers of makeup. "Why . . . I mean, how . . . this is just another one of your dirty tricks!"

Preposteror smiled triumphantly. "Well, we all have our little sources of information."

Tyrannia gulped, and then admitted meekly, "All right, since you already know . . . I had known for a long time who inherited the other half, namely, your third cousin, the film star Megaera Mummy in Hollywood. She always needed inordinate amounts of money because of her luxurious way of life; that's why I was able to purchase the scroll from her—for a horrific sum, though."

"That's better," said Preposteror. "Now we're getting down to brass tacks. However, I fear that you've been taken to the cleaners. Anything coming from that area is rarely authentic."

"What's that supposed to mean?"

"That you can be pretty sure that it's not the original, but just another one of those remakes."

"It is the original, you can bet on it!"

"Have you ever shown it to a specialist? Let me examine it."

He suddenly got a shifty look in his eyes.

His aunt answered with pursed lips, "You show me yours, and I'll show you mine."

"You know what," said Preposteror indifferently, "I don't really care one way or the other. You keep your half and I'll keep mine."

That did the trick.

His aunt tore the gigantic hat off her head and started pulling a long scroll of parchment out of its enormous brim. So that was why she had on that ridiculous headgear! Incidentally, now one could also see that she had but a few tufts of hair, dyed a bright red, which were rolled up into a skimpy, onion-shaped bun on top of her head.

"It *is* the original," she repeated grimly, presenting her nephew with the torn end.

Preposteror bent forward, adjusted his glasses, and could see immediately by the unusual lettering and other features that his aunt was, in fact, telling the truth.

He grabbed at it, but she pulled it away.

"Hands off, my boy! That's close enough."

"Hmmm," intoned Preposteror, stroking his chin, "it does appear to be the first part of the formula—but what's the formula for?"

Tyrannia wiggled around nervously on her chair. "I simply don't understand you, Beelzebub. Why are you asking so many questions? After all, ten thousand crowns is no chicken feed. Or are you just trying to jack up the price, you old cutthroat? Come on, how much do you want!"

Now she began conjuring further rolls of bank notes out of her pocketbook-safe.

Preposteror's bald dome was beaded with perspiration. "I wonder who's cutting whose throat here, dearest Auntie," he murmured. "So spit it out: what kind of formula is it?"

Tyrannia clenched her fat little fists. "Oh, a Black Friday to you and your nosiness! It's just an old recipe for punch. I'm quite simply in the mood for this particular punch this evening, because it's said to be most exquisite. Gourmets will be gourmets, we will pay any price for such a taste sensation, and I happen to have a sweet tooth."

"Come, come, Auntie," Preposteror replied with a shake of his head, "we both know that your sense of good taste abandoned you well over a hundred years ago. You can't tell the difference between raspberry juice and sulphuric acid. Who are you trying to kid, anyway?"

Tyrannia sprang to her feet, trembling with rage, and waddled about the laboratory. She had become increasingly fidgety during their negotiations, and had already snuck several peeks at the clock.

"All right already," she burst out suddenly, "I'll tell you, you thick-headed mule! But first you have to swear to me by Pluto's Deep Dark Treasury that you'll sell me your half of the scroll afterward."

The sorcerer grumbled a bit and executed an indefinable movement of the head, which could have been interpreted as a nod.

The witch pulled her chair up against his, sat down with a wheeze, and spoke in a subdued tone of voice. "Now listen carefully—it's the formula for the legendary Satanarchaeolidealcohellish Notion Potion. It is one of the most ancient and powerful evil spells in the universe. It works on New Year's Eve alone, because only then do wishes have an extra-special effect. Tonight is the middle night of the twelve nights between Christmas and Epiphany in which, as is well known, all the forces of darkness are unleashed. For every glass of this magic potion that you down in one gulp you get one wish, which is guaranteed to come true if you say it out loud."

Preposteror's eyes had glazed over during his aunt's explanation. The wheels were turning behind his forehead. His voice was suddenly hoarse with excitement as he asked, "Where in the name of Foul-and-Fatal-Fallout did you find all that out?"

"The directions are written at the beginning of the formula on my half of the scroll. There's no chance of a mistake."

A thousand stray thoughts crackled through the sorcerer's brain like the thunderbolts of an approaching storm. It suddenly dawned on him that this Notion Potion would make it possible for him to make up for all his omitted evil deeds—in one fell swoop, so to speak. That which lay suddenly so close and unexpected before him was his salvation! He would be able to outwit the hellish bailiff, after all. Of course, he would have to keep this marvelous hooch all to himself. By no means would he hand over his half of the parchment scroll to his aunt, no matter what she offered to pay. Quite to the contrary, it was imperative that he get his hands on hers, whatever the cost, even if he had to conjure her out of the world, or at least into another galaxy. Of course, that was easier thought than done. He was only too well aware of her

Michael Ende

Explanation of the word
SATANARCHAEOLIDEALCOHELLISH

This is one of those words which are frequently used in magic books and called *telescope words*, probably because they can be stretched out and squeezed together like telescopes in the olden days.

There are telescope words which stretch out over several lines, and sometimes even an entire page. In very rare cases they can cover a whole chapter. As a matter of fact, there was once supposedly a book which consisted of nothing but a single word-monster of this sort.

In sorcerers' and witches' circles, telescope words are thought of as particularly effective. The instructions you have to follow in order to make them are easy; the making itself, however, is difficult. This is because it must be possible to push the first or last syllable of a word over the first or last syllable of another word "in a straight or crooked way." Therefore, the words inside a long telescope word must fit into the preceding as well as the succeeding word.

In the present case, we are dealing with the following seven basic elements:

1. SATAN
2. ANARCH
3. ARCHAEOLOGY
4. LIE
5. IDEAL
6. ALCOHOL
7. HELLISH

These form six "simple" telescope words (single-jointed):

1. SATANARCH
2. ANARCHAEOLOGY
3. ARCHAEOLIE

4. LIDEAL
5. IDEALCOHOL
6. ALCOHELLISH

And these form five "double" telescope words (each double-jointed):

1. SATANARCHAEOLOGY
2. ANARCHAEOLIE
3. ARCHAEOLIDEAL
4. LIDEALCOHOL
5. IDEALCOHELLISH

Now these form four "triple" telescope words (each triple-jointed):

1. SATANARCHAEOLIE
2. ANARCHAEOLIDEAL
3. ARCHAEOLIDEALCOHOL
4. LIDEALCOHELLISH

These form three "double-double" telescope words (each quadruple-jointed):

1. SATANARCHAEOLIDEAL
2. ANARCHAEOLIDEALCOHOL
3. ARCHAEOLIDEALCOHELLISH

And these form the two "quinted" telescopic words (each quintuple-jointed):

1. SATANARCHAEOLIDEALCOHOL
2. ANARCHAEOLIDEALCOHELLISH

Which finally form the last "double-triple" telescope word (sextuple-jointed):

SATANARCHAEOLIDEALCOHELLISH

secret powers and knew that he had every reason to be very wary of her.

He stood up and started pacing back and forth, with his arms folded behind his back, so that she would not notice that his hands were shaking. He stopped, lost in thought, in front of the barrel marked TOXIC WASTE, drumming the rhythm of the latest hellish hit on the lid with his fingernails and humming to himself:

> "Dracula's blood began to curdle,
> When he saw little Rosie's girdle . . ."

The two animals inside the barrel ducked down, clung to each other, and held their breath. They had heard every word.

Preposteror turned suddenly and said, "I'm afraid it won't work, Tye—although it pains me to say so. You forgot one little thing, or rather two: the cat and the raven. They're going to want to be there, and since you have to say your wishes out loud, they'll hear everything. And then you'll have the High Council of Animals on your back. On the other hand, if we lock the two of them up or exclude them by force, it will raise just as many suspicions. It would be irresponsible of me to give you my half of the formula. I can't allow you to get involved in such a dangerous undertaking, dear Auntie."

Tyrannia flashed her gold teeth once again. "How sweet of you to be so worried about me, Bubby. But what you're saying is wrong. The cat and the raven are *supposed* to be there! In fact, I insist on their being witnesses. That's the best part of the whole thing."

The sorcerer drew nearer. "How do you mean?"

"We're not talking about just any magic potion here," explained the witch. "The Satanarchaeolidealcohellish Notion Potion boasts one ideal feature. It grants the *opposite* of everything you wish. You wish good health and you get a plague; you mention prosperity for all and actually cause misery; you say peace and the result is war. Now do you understand what a sweet little number this is, Bubby?"

Tyrannia chortled with pleasure and continued: "You know how much I love charity events. They are my great passion. Well, today I shall throw quite a party— no, wait, what am I saying?—a charity *orgy!*"

Preposteror's eyes began to sparkle behind the thick lenses of his glasses.

"Great radiating strontium!" he shouted. "And we'll even have the spies as witnesses that we only did our best—nothing but good deeds for this poor, suffering world!"

"This," cried Tyrannia, "will be a New Year's party the likes of which I've dreamed of since I first learned my money conjuror's one-times-one!"

And her nephew interjected in a bawling bass, "The world will remember this night for centuries to come —the night of the Great Catastrophe!"

"And no one will know where all the evil came from!" she screeched.

"Not a soul," he howled, "because you and I will be standing there as innocent as two little lambs, Tye!"

They fell into each other's arms and hopped about. The entire array of crucibles and test tubes in the room began playing a shrill, dissonant Waltz Macabre; the furniture kicked up its legs, the green flames in the fire-place flickered rhythmically, and even the stuffed shark on the wall snapped in time with its impressive teeth.

"Hey, catso," whispered Jacob, "I think I'm gonna be sick. My head feels so funny."

"Me too," Mauricio whispered back. "It's that music. We singers have very sensitive ears, you know."

"Maybe cats do," replied Jacob, "but no kind of music fazes the likes of us."

"Perhaps it's also due to the tranquillizers," said the little cat.

"Maybe in your case, but not in mine," murmured the raven. "Are you really sure that you understood what was written on the barrel?"

"Why?" asked Mauricio fearfully.

"Maybe this stuff we're squatting in is poisonous."

"What!? You think we're already contaminated?"

Horror-stricken, the little cat attempted to jump out of the barrel straightaway. Jacob held him back.

"Stop! Not yet! We've got to wait till those two are gone, or else all is lost."

"What if they don't go away?"

"Then this will come to no good end," the raven croaked glumly.

"Forgive me!" breathed the little cat remorsefully.

"What is there to forgive?"

"I can't really read at all."

There was a moment of silence, then Jacob croaked, "Oh, if only I had stayed back in the nest with Tamara."

"Is that yet another one?" asked Mauricio.

But Jacob did not reply.

The sorcerer and the witch had sunk down onto their chairs and were trying to catch their breath. Every now and then a wicked giggle escaped their lips. Preposteror wiped clean the fogged-over lenses of his glasses with the sleeve of his dressing gown; Tyrannia dabbed away the sweat from her upper lip daintily with a lace handkerchief, so as not to smudge her makeup.

"Oh, by the way, Bubby," she said casually, "you keep talking about 'we' and 'us.' Just so that we understand one another: I may need your half of the scroll and your expert advice, but you're getting more than well paid for services rendered, right? Naturally, *I'll* be the one doing the drinking and wishing. You're not in on that."

"Wrong, Auntie," replied Preposteror. "You'd only end up going on an alcohellish bender, and possibly getting sick. After all, you're no spring chicken anymore. Better leave that part of it to me. You can always tell me what I should wish for you. I'll only play along under that condition."

Tyrannia hit the roof. "I can't believe my ears!" she bellowed. "You swore by Pluto's Deep Dark Treasury that you'd sell me your half."

Preposteror rubbed his hands together. "Really? I don't seem to remember any such thing."

"For Devil's sake, Bubby," she gasped, "you're not going to break your solemn oath, are you?"

"I didn't swear anything," he answered with a grin. "You must be hearing things."

"Whatever has become of our good old family spirit," she exclaimed, covering her face with her ring-laden hands, "if even an unsuspecting old aunt can't trust her favorite nephew anymore!"

"Come, come, Tye," Preposteror said. "Are you starting up with that hogwash again?"

They traded hostile looks for a while.

"If we keep this up," the witch pronounced finally, "we'll still be sitting here next year."

She cast another glance at the clock, and it was clear that she was having a lot of trouble keeping a grip on herself. Her hanging cheeks trembled and her several double chins quivered.

Preposteror secretly relished the situation—although he didn't feel much better himself. He had been dependent on the money witch for so many long years—and she had let him know it—that it was now an outright pleasure to really let her have it.

He would gladly have stretched out the game a little longer, yet he himself had but a few short hours till midnight.

"The New Year will be here soon," he murmured absentmindedly.

"You said it," Tyrannia burst out, "and do you know what happens then, you fool? The Notion Potion loses its reversing power at the first stroke of the New Year's bells!"

"You're exaggerating as usual, Tye," Preposteror ventured, slightly disconcerted. "I can't stand the New Year's bells either, because they always give me heartburn, but you're not trying to tell me that the ring of a bell can take away the entire infernal magic power of so awesome a potion."

"Not the magic power," she snorted, "the *reversing power*—and that is much worse! Then the lie becomes truth, do you understand?! Then everything you wished for is taken literally."

"Wait a minute," said the sorcerer, confused, "what's that supposed to mean?"

"That means that we absolutely have to have finished brewing up the potion before midnight, and as long before midnight as possible. I have to have drunk every drop and made every wish before the first stroke of the New Year sounds. If so much as the tiniest bit remains, everything will go wrong! Imagine what will happen then: all my seemingly good wishes, including the ones I made at the start, would no longer be turned around but would literally come true."

"How horrible!" groaned Preposteror. "How revolting! How atrocious! How ghastly!"

"You see!" confirmed his aunt. "But if we hurry, we can expect the best."

"The best?" Preposteror's face twitched in confusion. "What do you mean by the best?"

"Naturally I mean the worst," she said, placating him. "The best for us, but in reality the worst. The worst we could possibly wish for."

"How wonderful!" Preposteror cried. "How fabulous! How marvelous! How splendiferous!"

"You said it, my boy," Tyrannia replied, giving him an encouraging slap on the knee. "So get on the ball, will you!"

When she saw that her nephew was still staring at her hesitatingly, she once again pulled more rolls of bank notes out of her pocketbook-safe and piled them up in front of him. "Perhaps that'll get the wheels turning again in that head of yours. Here you are, twenty thousand—fifty—eighty—one hundred thousand! But that is absolutely my final offer. Now go and bring me your half of the scroll! Quick! Run! Or else I might change my mind."

Yet Preposteror did not budge.

He had absolutely no idea whether his aunt would refrain from carrying out her threat, or whether he was risking everything with this final bluff, but he had to take the chance.

With a stony face he said, "Keep your money, Auntie Tye. It doesn't interest me."

Now the witch flipped her lid. Gasping with exertion, she threw roll after roll of bank notes at him and screamed madly, "There, there, and there . . . What else should I offer you? How much more do you want, you hyena? A million? Three? Five? Ten? . . ."

She dipped both hands into the mountain of bills and

threw it in the air like a madwoman, so that bills fluttered down all over the laboratory.

At last she collapsed onto her chair in exhaustion and panted, "Whatever is the matter with you, Beelzebubby? You used to be so greedy and corruptible and generally such a nice, obedient boy. Whatever changed you so?"

"It's no use, Tye," he said. "Either you give me your half of the scroll—or else you finally admit why you're so desperate to have mine."

"Who? Me?" she asked weakly, in a last attempt at playing dumb. "Why? What should it matter to me? It's only for a simple New Year's Eve joke."

"I'm afraid I don't think it's funny," said Preposteror coldly. "Our senses of humor are too different, dearest Auntie. I guess we had better forget all this nonsense. Let's just drop it! Perhaps you'd like a nice cup of hemlock tea?"

Yet, instead of gratefully accepting this polite offer, Tyrannia went into a temper tantrum. She turned quince-yellow beneath her piglet-colored makeup, let loose an inarticulate cry reminiscent of a whistling buoy, jumped up, and stamped her feet like an irate child.

Now, we know that such outbursts have completely different results with witches and sorcerers than with irate children. The floor ripped open with a crackle of thunder, flames and smoke pouring forth from the rent along with the head of a giant, glowing-red camel perched on a snake-like neck, which opened its mouth and bleated at the Shadow Sorcery Minister with ear-splitting intensity.

Yet the latter did not seem in the least impressed.

"I beg of you, Auntie," he said wearily, "you're only ruining my floorboards—and my eardrums."

Tyrannia made a sign for the camel to disappear, the floor closed up again without leaving a trace, and now the witch flabbergasted the sorcerer after all with something unexpected.

She wept.

That is, she pretended to, for witches cannot shed real tears, of course. Still, she sucked in her face like a dried-up lemon, dabbed her eyes with her lace handkerchief, and whined, "Oh, Bubby, you naughty, naughty boy! Why must you always upset me so? You know how temperamental I am."

Preposteror looked at her with loathing. "Embarrassing" was all he said. "Really most embarrassing."

She tried out a few more halfhearted sobs, but then she stopped the show and declared in a defeated voice. "All right; if I tell you, you'll have me in your clutches one hundred percent—and naturally, I know you, you'll exploit that shamelessly. But what the hell, I'm lost either way. Today I was visited by a hellish official, one Maledictus Maggot, dispatched by my benefactor, Infernal Secretary of the Treasury Mammon. He told me that I would be personally foreclosed upon tonight at the turn of the New Year. And that is all your fault, Beelzebub Preposteror! As your employer I am in the sourest of pickles now. Just because *you* were way behind with *your*

work, *I* got into arrears with my business and couldn't wreak as much havoc as stated in my contract. And now the Deepest Circles down there are on my back. They're holding me responsible! That's what I get for financing my lazy, incompetent nephew out of devotion to the family! If you had just a speck of a guilty conscience in you, you would give me your half of the formula on the spot so that I could drink the Notion Potion. It's my last resort. Or else, may you be cursed with the most evil curse of all: the Curse of the Rich Relations!"

Preposteror had unfolded his entire spindly length into a standing position. During Tyrannia's speech the tip of his nose had gradually taken on a greenish tinge.

"Desist!" he cried, and held up his hand. "Desist before you do something you might regret! If what you have said is true, then we have no other choice but to join forces. We're in each other's clutches now, dear Auntie. That hellish bailiff visited me as well and I am also to be foreclosed upon at midnight, unless I make good on my contract. We're sitting in the same boat, my dearest, and we can either rescue ourselves or go down together."

Tyrannia had stood up as well while he was speaking. She looked at her nephew and held out her arms. "Bubby," she stammered, "I could kiss you!"

"Later, later," Preposteror said evasively. "We've got more urgent business at hand. The two of us shall begin preparing this legendary Satanarchaeolidealcohellish Notion Potion without any further ado; then the two of us shall drink it, taking turns, one glass for you, one glass for me; and all the while the two of us shall make our wishes, first me, then you, then me again—"

"No," his aunt interrupted, "first *me*, then *you*."

"We can draw straws," he suggested.

"Fine with me," she said.

They each thought that they would certainly find a way of cheating the other later on. And each of them knew that the other was thinking the same thing. They were, after all, members of the same family.

"Well then, I'll go and get my half of the formula," Preposteror said.

"And I'll go along with you, Bubby," Tyrannia answered. "Trust is one thing, control is another, don't you agree?"

Preposteror rushed off and Tyrannia followed after with surprising nimbleness.

As soon as their steps had faded away, the little cat came tumbling out of the barrel. He felt dizzy and miserable. The raven, who wasn't feeling any better, fluttered after him.

"Well," he croaked, "did you hear everything?"

"Yes," said Mauricio.

"And do you understand what's happening?"

"No," said Mauricio.

"But I do," declared the raven, "so who wins the bet?"

"You do," said Mauricio.

"And how about that rusty nail, comrade? Who has to swallow it?"

"I do," said Mauricio, adding somewhat theatrically, "So be it! I want to die anyway."

"Nonsense!" croaked Jacob. "It was just for fun. Forget it! The main thing is that now you're convinced I was right."

"That's just why I want to die," Mauricio said tragically. "No chivalrous minnesinger can bear such shame. It's nothing you would understand."

"Oh, why don't you just drop your highfalutin airs!" Jacob said angrily. "You can always die later. We've got more important things to do now." And he stalked about the laboratory on his skinny legs.

"You're right, I'll postpone it for a while," agreed Mauricio, "because first I wish to give that unscrupulous villain, whom I used to call Maestro, a piece of my mind. I shall spit my disdain into his face. I want him to know—"

"You'll do no such thing," said Jacob. "Or do you want to spoil everything all over again?"

Mauricio's eyes glowed with fiery determination.

"I'm not afraid. I must give vent to my outrage, otherwise I could never look myself in the eye again. I want him to know what Mauricio di Mauro thinks of him . . ."

"Sure," said Jacob dryly, "that's really going to bother him. Now listen to me for once, you heroic tenor! By no means are the two of them to suspect that we know what they're up to."

"Why not?" asked the little cat.

"Because as long as they don't know that we know, we might be able to foil their plans. Do you get it?"

"Foil them? How?"

"Well . . . for example . . . oh, how do I know. We have to make sure that they don't get their magic hooch done on time. We could do something clumsy like knock over the glass with the hooch in it, or . . . Well, we'll think of something. We just have to be on our talons."

"On our what?"

"Kid, you really don't understand anything. We have to keep our eyes open, get it? We have to watch every move they make. And that's why the two of them mustn't notice that we were eavesdropping. That's the only advantage we have left, comrade. Is our flight pattern finally clear?"

He fluttered up onto the table.

"I see!" said Mauricio. "That means that the future of the world now lies in our paws."

"More or less," said the raven, while stalking among the papers, "although I wouldn't exactly say paws."

Mauricio puffed up his chest and murmured, "Ho, a great deed . . . destiny beckons . . . a noble knight knows no fear . . ."

He was trying to remember the rest of the famous cat aria when Jacob suddenly croaked, "Hey, get over here!"

He had discovered Tyrannia's scroll, which she had left lying on the table, and was peering at it, first with one eye, then with the other.

The little cat was at his side with one leap.

"Look, look!" the raven whispered hoarsely. "If we was to throw this thing into the fire, then that would be the end of the magic potion. Your Maestro said himself that the second half alone is useless to him."

"I knew it!" cried Mauricio. "I was sure we would have a marvelous idea. Quick, away with it! And when those villains start to look for it, we shall step up to them and say—"

" 'Twas the wind," Jacob interrupted him. "That's what we'll say—if we say anything at all. The best thing is, we don't know anything. Do you think I feel like having my neck wrung by the two of them to wind things up?"

"You're just a philistine, after all," said Mauricio disenchantedly. "You simply have no sense of greatness."

"You said it," agreed Jacob. "That's why I'm still alive. Come on, give me a hand!"

They were just about to grab the scroll when, suddenly, the snake of parchment uncoiled of its own accord and raised its front end high, like a giant cobra swaying to a flute player.

The two
heroes'
hearts sank
immediately
into their talons
—or rather, paws.
They clung together
and looked up at the
swaying tip of the scroll,
which seemed to be staring
down at them menacingly.

"Do you think it bites?"
Mauricio whispered quakingly.

"How do I know," said Jacob,
his beak clattering lightly.

And before they knew what
was happening, the scroll had
wrapped itself around them with a
lightning movement, again and
again, until it looked like a parcel
with a cat's and a raven's head
sticking out at the top. The two of
them could not move a muscle and
could hardly breathe. The scroll
wound tighter and tighter.

They fought with all

their fading strength, but the parchment could not be torn.

"Gasp! Puff! Ugh!" was all they could manage to utter.

At which point Preposteror's hoarse bass resounded.

"Unruly spook,
By your master's ring,
Unwrap your cocoon
From those nosy things!"

At that very moment the snake scroll came tumbling down, twitched once or twice, and then lay motionless—nothing more than a long, bescrawled strip of parchment.

"Most humble thanks, Your High and Mightiness," panted Jacob. "That was close!"

Mauricio couldn't speak at all, first because every bone in his body ached, and second because the cat had got his tongue—for it was Preposteror of all people who had saved their lives; Preposteror, whom he had actually meant to punish with deepest disdain. Mauricio's intellect was no match for such complications.

Now Tyrannia Vampirella appeared behind the sorcerer.

"Holy profit!" she cried. "You poor little things, you didn't hurt yourselves, did you?" She stroked the raven's head.

The sorcerer stroked Mauricio and said in a benevolent voice, "Now listen, this is not a toy store! You should know better, Mauricio di Mauro. You must never touch anything without my express permission. It's much too dangerous. All manner of things could happen to you, and that would make your dear Maestro very, very sad."

"Blablabla . . ." the raven croaked almost inaudibly to himself.

The sorcerer and the witch exchanged a quick glance, and then she asked, "Jacoboo, my dear raven, what are you doing here, anyway?"

"If you please, madam," said Jacob innocently, "I just came to announce your visit."

"Really? I can't seem to remember having ordered you to do so, my little pigeon."

"I came on my own, because I thought you just wanted to spare me, because you were worried about the filthy weather and my rawmatism, but I was just dying to do you a favor."

"Well, that's very sweet of you, Jacoboo. But from now on, you had better ask first."

"Did I do the wrong thing again?" asked the raven shamefacedly. "Oh, I'm such a sad sack of feathers."

"Say," said the sorcerer, turning to the cat, "where have you two been hiding, you little rascals?"

Mauricio was about to reply, but the raven butted in hastily. "That disgusting bird-eater tried to drag me into his chamber, Your High and Mightiness, but I got away and zipped down into the cellar, but he caught me anyway and locked me up in a stinking old crate, and I complained for hours, because that's no good manners and that's not no way to treat a guest, and then he unlocked the crate and said I should keep my beak shut or else he would roast me in the oven like a turkey, and so I gave him one on the noggin and then we engaged in fisticuffs, and before you know it, we were back here, don't ask me how, and during the scuffle that stupid paper snake wrapped itself around us, and then you came, lucky for us. But I really must say this cat belongs in a cage, that's where he belongs, because he's a surefire public danger and a bloodthirsty beast!"

Mauricio had been listening to the raven's outburst in wide-eyed wonder. He had tried to interrupt a few times but, as luck would have it, without success. Now Preposteror addressed him laughingly: "Well done, my brave little knight! But from now on, you two have to get along. Do you both promise?"

"Well, pluck my feathers!" croaked Jacob, turning his back on Mauricio. "How can I get along with someone who calls me a turkey? First he has to take that back!"

"But—" Mauricio protested, before the witch interrupted him.

"No buts!" she piped in a sickeningly sweetish voice. "Be nice to each other, you little scoundrels! You see, my wonderful nephew and I have thought up something extra-special for you. And if you are nice and friendly and get along well, you may join in our New Year's Eve celebration. It should be a lot of fun, don't you think, Bubby?"

"You can say that again," Preposteror said with a crooked grin. "You're really in for something. If you're good."

"It rubs my feathers the wrong way," rasped Jacob, "but if there's no other way, we'll make a truce. Baron, what do you say?"

He nudged Mauricio with his wing, and the latter nodded a little foolishly.

In the meantime, the witch had rolled up the snake scroll. Now the sorcerer produced a similar-looking scroll from within the wide sleeve of his dressing gown.

"First of all, Tye," he explained, "we have to put to the test whether the two halves in fact originally belonged together. You know the spell and what you have to do?"

"All clear," she said.

Then they spoke together:

> "By the power of six-and-sixty
> Pentagrams all in a row,
> Prove these parts be part and party
> Of the one and only scroll.
> Formula of deepest night,
> If it's you, then show your might!
> Join what once was rent asunder,
> To the sound of flames and thunder!
> Ready! Set! Go!"

The two of them threw their parchment scrolls into the air at the same moment. There was a huge, blinding flash of lightning and the air all around sparkled with thousands of little stars, like a display of fireworks, but this time not a sound could be heard.

The two halves had shot together and become one, as if under the influence of a colossal magnetic force—and they were as perfectly joined as if they had never been separated, with no sign of a rip.

A snake scroll of approximately five yards length floated in long, slow waves back and forth beneath the ceiling of the laboratory, sinking bit by bit to the floor.

The Night of Wishes

The sorcerer and the witch nodded at each other in satisfaction.

"And now you have to leave us alone for a little while," said Preposteror, turning to the animals. "We want to prepare our New Year's Eve party and you'll just be in the way."

Jacob, who still had the secret intention of preventing the timely completion of the Notion Potion, begged and pleaded to be allowed to stay, promising to be very, very quiet. Mauricio joined in.

"Not a chance, you little rubbernecks," said Tyrannia. "You would just keep bothering us with your questions—and besides, it is supposed to be a surprise for you."

All their coaxing was in vain, and finally, the witch grabbed the raven and the sorcerer the cat. They carried them into Mauricio's chamber and put them down.

"Why don't you two catch a few winks in advance," said Preposteror, "so you won't get sleepy later on at the party. Especially you, kitty."

"Or you can play woolball to pass the time," added Tyrannia. "The main thing is to be good and not fight anymore. When we're done we'll come and get you."

"And just to make sure that you don't peek and spoil all the fun for us and yourselves," Preposteror continued, "we'll lock you in till then."

He closed the door and turned the key in the lock. Their steps faded away.

Michael Ende

Jacob Scribble fluttered onto the arm of the old plush sofa, several springs of which were protruding out of the cushions where the cat had sharpened his claws once too often.

"Well," he rasped bitterly, "now we're in a fine mess, we two super spies, and a silly mess at that."

The first thing Mauricio had done was to run to his luxurious canopy bed, but then, although he felt more tired and sick than ever in his life, he had made the heroic decision not to lie down. The situation was too serious to consider a catnap.

"What are we going to do now?" he asked perplexedly.

"What're we going to do now?" croaked Jacob. "We're going to be a sorry sight, no more, no less! So much for foiling their plans.

The Night of Wishes

"I said it first,
things always keep going
from worser to worst.

"And that's the truth of it, because rhymes don't lie. This will come to no good end!"

"Why do you keep saying that?" Mauricio complained.

"That's my fillosophy," explained Jacob. "One must generally expect the worst and then do what one can to prevent it."

"And what *can* we do?" asked Mauricio.

"Nothin'," Jacob admitted.

Mauricio was standing in front of the low coffee table, enticingly decked out with saucers of sweet cream and various tasty tidbits. Although it took enormous self-control, he resisted this temptation as well, since he now knew the disastrous effect this catnip would have on him.

It was quiet for a while, with only the sound of the blizzard whistling around the house.

"I'll tell you something, kitty"—the raven finally broke the silence—"I'm fed up with the secret agent profession. This goes way beyond the call of duty. I'm at the end of my feather. I've had it. I'm quitting."

"Now of all times?" asked Mauricio. "But you can't do that!"

"Oh yes, I can," said Jacob. "I'm sick of it. I'd like to lead a perfectly normal vagabond life again, like in

the olden days. I wish I was in my warm nest with Ramona."

Mauricio sat down and looked up at him. "Ramona? Why Ramona all of a sudden?"

"Because she is farthest away," said the woebegone Jacob, "and that's where I'd most like to be now."

"You know," Mauricio said after a short pause, "I would also much rather wander through foreign lands and melt all hearts with my songs. But if those two villains destroy the world tonight with their magic, what kind of life will be left for a minnesinger, if there is any life left at all?"

"So what?" croaked Jacob angrily. "What can we do about it? We two lousy, pitiful creatures, of all animals? Why doesn't anyone else bother—up there in heaven, for example? There's one thing I'd like to know: why do the bad guys in the world always have so much power and the good guys never have anything—except maybe rawmatism? It's not fair, kitty. No, it's just not fair! I'm sick of it. I'm going on strike, that's all there is to it."

And with that he stuck his head under his wing so as no longer to see or hear anything.

This time it was quiet for such a long time that he finally peeked out from under his wing and said, "The least you could do is contradict me."

"I must think about what you said before," said Mauricio. "With me it's just the other way around. My great-grandmother Mia, who was a very wise old feline, always used to say: If you can get excited about some-

thing, then do it—and if you can't, then go to sleep. I
have to be able to get excited, which is why I always
try to picture the best of all possibilities and then to do
all I can to achieve *it*. But unfortunately, I haven't as
much experience and common sense as you, or else I
would most certainly come up with a way out of this."

The raven pulled his head from under his wing, open-
ing his beak and closing it again. This unexpected com-
pliment coming from a famous artist of ancient, noble
lineage left him speechless. No such thing had ever happened to him in his entire, shady raven's life.

He cleared his throat. "Hm, well," he croaked, "one
thing's for sure, nothing is going to happen as long as

we're sitting in here. We've got to get out. The question is how. The door is locked. Any ideas?"

"Maybe I can open the window," Mauricio suggested eagerly.

"Try it!"

"What for?"

"We've got a journey ahead of us—quite a long journey, probably."

"Where to?"

"To get help."

"Help? You mean the High Council?"

"No, it's already too late for that. By the time we got there and they could do anything, midnight would have

come and gone. There's no point to any of that anymore."

"Who else can possibly help us?"

Jacob scratched his head pensively with his claw. "I don't know. A miracle is probably the only thing that can help us now. Maybe fate will have a heart—although experience tells me we shouldn't really rely on it. But we can give it a try."

"That's not much," said Mauricio meekly. "I can't really get excited about that."

Jacob nodded gloomily. "You're right. After all, it's warmer in here. But as long as we sit around, we don't even have the chintz of a chance."

Mauricio reflected for a moment; then he pulled himself together, leaped onto the sill, and, with some effort, opened the window.

Snow swirled into the room.

"Let's go!" croaked the raven, and fluttered out. He was immediately caught up by a gust of wind and disappeared somewhere in the darkness.

The fat little cat gathered all his courage and leaped in pursuit. He fell a long ways and plopped into a snowbank, which closed in over him. Only with great effort could he scramble free.

"Jacob Scribble, where are you?" he meowed fearfully.

"Here!" he heard the raven's voice nearby.

It is essential to all forms of magic not only that you know the right formulas, have the right paraphernalia at your disposal, and carry out the right action at the right time, but also that you be in the right frame of mind. Your mood must correspond to the task you have set yourself. This, by the way, is just as true of evil magic as it is of the good variety (which certainly exists as well, even if it is probably rarer nowadays). To do good magic, you have to put yourself in a loving, harmonious mood, and to do evil magic, in a wild and hateful one. Each case requires a certain amount of preparation.

And that is exactly what the sorcerer and the witch were preoccupied with.

The laboratory shone in the cool glow of countless electric spotlights and lamps, both large and small, which quivered, flickered, and flashed from all corners.

The room was couched in swaths of fog, for thick, multicolored clouds billowed out of several incense basins, creeping along the floor and up the walls and assuming all manner of faces and grimaces, large and small, which instantly dissolved, only to reappear at once in another form.

Preposteror sat at his organ, hitting the keys with grandiose gestures. The pipes of the instrument consisted of the bones of animals which had been tortured to death; the smallest were little chicken legs, the larger ones from seals, dogs, and apes, and the largest from elephants and whales.

Aunt Tyrannia stood beside him and turned the pages of his score. It sounded pretty grim when they began singing the Chorale No. CO_2 from *Satan's Hymnbook*:

> Cursed be you, sense and reason,
> Evil is the light of day.
> Free the soul from your foul treason.
> Truth and wisdom, go away!
>
> May my words ring true with lies,
> Raining down from test-tube skies.
> False is what the world shall be,
> And reality shall flee.
>
> Order shall not find our favor,
> Of nature, nor of intellect.
> Chaos is the favorite flavor
> On a menu of disrespect.

The Night of Wishes

Since our conscience bogs us down,
Our powers lift us off the ground.
If all barriers fall away,
While the sun shines, we'll make hay.

An oath we swear of deadly
Destruction from the very start.
Nonsensical insanity
Is our science, is our art!

And after every strophe there followed the refrain:

Evil potion do we mix.
Blackest magic, do your tricks!

This was all done to get into the proper mood. No
wonder they did not want the animals to witness it. In
any case, the sorcerer and the witch were now in the
right frame of mind for their creation.

"First of all," explained Preposteror, "we must make
the proper container for the Satanarchaeolidealcohellish
Notion Potion."

"Make it?" asked Tyrannia. "Don't you even have a
potion tureen in this bachelor pad of yours?"

"Dearest Auntie," said Preposteror condescendingly,
"you really don't have the foggiest notion about alcohellish drinks. No potion tureen in the world—even if
it had been cut from a single diamond—could withstand

the procedure necessary for producing this potion. It would burst or melt or simply evaporate."

"So what are we going to do?"

The sorcerer smiled patronizingly. "Ever heard of Cold Fire?"

Tyrannia shook her head.

"Well, pay attention," said Preposteror. "You might learn something, Tye."

He went over to a shelf and took out a kind of over-sized spray can, then moved to the fireplace, in which the fire blazed up at that very moment. While spraying something invisible into the flames, he spoke the following words:

> "Imagery of flickering flame,
> Of fire that spits and smokes,
> Your feverish dance is but a game
> And time reveals the hoax.
> Salamander coat of luster,
> By the power of anti-clock,
> Imagery of fiery bluster,
> Turn as cold and hard as rock!"

Right away the fire stopped flickering and stood still—completely motionless—and now looked like some strange, large plant with many glowing-green, jagged leaves.

Preposteror reached in with his bare hands and plucked off one leaf after another, until he had an armful.

He had barely finished when a new fire flared up in the hearth and danced as before.

The sorcerer went to the table in the middle of the laboratory, where he fitted together the rigid, glassy-green leaves like the pieces of a puzzle. Where the jagged edges fit perfectly together, they melted into a single piece in no time (the variously shaped flames in *every* fire would always form a whole—if brought together —only these forms are constantly changing, and changing so quickly that one cannot observe them with the normal eye).

A flat dish quickly materialized beneath Preposteror's skilled hands; then he added sides, until, finally, a large, round goldfish bowl approximately three feet tall and three feet wide stood there. It glowed with a greenish light and looked somehow unreal.

"Well," said the sorcerer, wiping his fingers on his dressing gown, "that's that. Looks good, don't you think?"

"And you think it's going to hold?" asked the witch. "Guaranteed?"

"You can bet on it."

"Beelzebub Preposteror," said Tyrannia with a mixture of envy and respect, "how did you do that?"

"You would hardly be able to grasp such scientific processes, Auntie," Preposteror said. "Heat and movement exist only in positive time. If one sprinkles them with negative moments, so-called anti-time particles, they cancel each other out and the fire becomes rigid and cold, as you just saw."

"Can you touch it?"

"Naturally."

The witch let her hand glide cautiously over the surface of the giant bowl. Then she asked, "Could you teach me how to do that, Bubby?"

Preposteror shook his head. "Professional secret!"

The Dead Park surrounding the Villa Nightmare was not particularly big. Although it was in the center of town, hardly anyone in the neighborhood had ever seen it, for it was surrounded by a stone wall nine feet high.

But sorcerers can also construct invisible obstacles which, for example, are composed of Forget or Sad or Confused. Thus had Preposteror constructed an invisible barrier of Fear and Horror around his property beyond the stone wall, which prompted all busybodies to continue hastily on their way, rather than bothering about what was behind the wall.

There was one high gate of rusted wrought iron, but even here one could not peek into the park, since the view was blocked by a dense, tangled hedge of giant black thorns. This was the gate Preposteror used when he took a ride in his Magimobile—which was a rare occurrence indeed.

Once upon a time—when it still had another name—the Dead Park had consisted of a mass of big, beautiful trees and picturesque clusters of bushes, but now they were all bare—and not only because it was winter. The sorcerer had carried out his scientific experiments on them for decades, had manipulated their growth, crippled their regenerative powers, and tapped their life sources until he had slowly tortured them to death, one after the other. Now they merely stretched thin, withered branches into the sky, as if they had cried for help with agonized gestures before they died—but no one had heard their silent cry. There had not been a bird in the park for a long time, not even in summer.

The fat little cat trudged through the deep snow, with the raven hopping and fluttering beside him, although he got blown over by the wind from time to time. Both were silent, for they needed all their strength to fight their way forward.

The high stone wall would have been no problem for Jacob, but it definitely was for Mauricio. But then he remembered the iron gate through which he had first entered. They squeezed through the ornate iron bars.

The invisible barrier of Fear was no great problem for them either, since it had been specially constructed for people and was made of Fear of Ghosts; even die-hard skeptics suddenly believed in ghosts when they entered this zone, and took to their heels.

Most animals are afraid of ghosts as well—but cats and ravens least of all.

"Tell me, Jacob," asked Mauricio quietly, "do you believe in ghosts?"

"Sure," said Jacob.

"Have you ever seen one?"

"Not personally," said Jacob, "but in the olden days all my relatives used to squat on the gallows where the hanged men swung. Or they nested on the roofs of haunted castles. In any case, there were ghosts galore, there were. But the likes of us never had any trouble with them. Not that I know of. On the contrary, some of them were good friends of my people."

"Yes," said Mauricio bravely, "it was just the same with my ancestors."

In this way they had passed through the invisible barrier and were now on the street.

The windows of the high buildings were festively illuminated, for people everywhere were celebrating New Year's Eve or preparing for the joyous event. Hardly a car was still on the road, and rarer still was the sight of a pedestrian, hat pulled low, hurriedly heading somewhere or other.

No one in the entire town had any idea of the catastrophe that was brewing in the Villa Nightmare. And no one noticed the fat little cat and the tattered raven who had made their way into the unknown to search for salvation.

At first, the two of them wondered whether they shouldn't just appeal to one of the passersby, but they quickly changed their minds, for first of all, it was highly unlikely that a normal person would understand their meowing and croaking (it was possible that he would only take them and lock them in a cage), and second of all, they knew that there was hardly ever any hope of success when animals asked people for help. This had been proven often enough. Even when it was in their own interest to pay heed to nature's cries for help, humans had remained deaf. People had seen the bloody tears of many animals—and still gone on as before.

No, there was no hope of a split-second rescue at the hands of the humans. At whose hands, then? Jacob and Mauricio couldn't say. They just kept on going and going. It was a little easier walking on the plowed street, yet their progress was still slow against the snowstorm blowing into their faces. But, of course, those who know not where they are headed are not in much of a hurry.

After they had gone on side by side for some time, Mauricio said quietly, "Jacob, perhaps these are our last hours in this life. Therefore, I absolutely must tell you something. I never would have thought that I would become friends with a bird someday, let alone with a raven, but now I am proud that I have found such a wise and experienced friend as yourself. Truly, I do admire you."

The raven cleared his throat in slight embarrassment and then replied in a husky voice, "I'd have never thought myself that I would ever have a real chum who's a famous artist and a proper dandy to boot. I don't know just how to put it. No one never taught me good manners and fancy words. You see, I'm just a common, run-of-the-mill vagabond, here today, gone tomorrow, and I've always managed to get along somehow. I'm not as educated as you. The windblown ravens' nest where I crawled out of the egg was a common, run-of-the-mill ravens' nest, and my parents were common, run-of-the-mill, raving raven parents—very common, for that matter. No one has ever really liked me, not even myself. And I'm not musical, that's for sure. And I never learned no pretty songs. But I imagine it's great if you can."

"Oh, Jacob, Jacob," cried the little cat, who had trouble not showing that he was close to tears, "I do not stem from an ancient lineage of knights, and my ancestors didn't come from Naples. To tell the truth, I'm not even quite sure where that is. And my name isn't Mauricio di Mauro either; I just made that up. My real name is Morris—plain old Morris. At least you know who your parents were—I don't even know that much, because I grew up among stray, wild cats in some damp hole of a cellar. They took turns at being mother, one day one, the next day the other, whoever felt like it. The other kittens were all much stronger than I when it came to getting their share of the catnip. That's why I remained so small and my appetite so big. And I certainly never was a famous minnesinger. I never did have a beautiful voice."

Both were silent for a while.

"Well, why did you say so in the first place?" Jacob asked pensively.

The cat pondered on it.

"I don't really know," he admitted. "It was my life's dream, do you understand? I so wished to become a famous artist—big and beautiful and elegant, with a silky white coat and a wonderful voice. Someone everybody loves and respects."

"Hmm," said Jacob.

"It was just a dream," continued the little cat, "and actually, I always knew that it would never come true. That's why I simply pretended that it was so. Do you think that was a big sin?"

"How do I know," rasped Jacob. "I don't know anything about sins and pious stuff like that."

"Yes, but . . . are you angry with me now?"

"Angry? Nonsense—I think you're a little soft in the head. But that doesn't matter. You're still all right."

And the raven put his tattered wing around his friend's shoulders for the space of a moment.

"When I think about it," he said, "the name Morris doesn't not please me half bad; quite to the contrary."

"No, I mean because I am not a famous singer, after all."

"Who knows," said the raven enigmatically. "I have known lies to become truths with time—and then they were lies no more."

Morris cast a somewhat uneasy sideways glance at his

traveling companion, because he hadn't quite understood what Jacob meant.

"Do you think I could still become one?" he asked with widened eyes.

"If we live long enough . . ." said Jacob, half to himself.

The little cat continued excitedly: "I told you about Grandma Mia, didn't I, the wise old cat who knew so many mysterious things? She also lived with us in the cellar. She has been with the Great Tom in Kitty Heaven for a long time now, like all the others, except for me. Shortly before she died, she told me something. 'Morris,' she said, 'if you really want to become a great artist, you must experience all of life's ups and downs, for only he who has done so can touch the hearts of one and all.' Yes, that is what she said. But do you understand what she meant?"

"Well," answered the raven dryly, "you've already experienced the downs, I should say."

"Do you really think so?" asked Morris happily.

"Sure," croaked Jacob. "You can't get any lower than rock bottom, kitty. Now all you need are the ups."

And they continued on in silence through the snow and the wind.

Far off at the end of the street the steeple of the cathedral stood out against the nighttime sky.

In the meantime, the work in the laboratory was in full swing.

The first step was to gather the various substances necessary for the production of the Satanarchaeolideal-cohellish Notion Potion. The long strip of parchment lay unrolled on the floor and was weighted down with piles of books so it wouldn't roll up again.

Having once more carefully studied the instructions at the beginning of the scroll, Preposteror and Tyrannia now got down to the formula itself. Both stood hunched over the text, deciphering what was written there. This would have been impossible for non-sorcerers, for they were dealing with an incredibly complicated secret alphabet, the so-called Infernal Code. But for the two of them, cracking the code was a piece of cake. Also, the requirements concerning the basic ingredients were still relatively uncomplicated at the beginning.

Translated into our alphabet, the beginning of the formula read as follows:

> Rivers four do flow through hell,
> Darkest torture's sacred well:
> The Cocytus, the Acheron,
> The Styx and Pyriphlegethon.
> Ice, fire, poison, slime,
> Take a pinch of all four kinds,
> Shake it up over the sink,
> Basis for a lying drink.

Like all well-equipped lab sorcerers, Preposteror had sufficient supplies of all four substances. While he gathered and mixed them reverently in a special shaker, Tyrannia read the next part out loud:

> "Liquid money's what you need:
> Put ten grand in your account,
> Stockpiled from a lifetime's greed
> And stolen to a large amount.
> Liquefy the interest only—
> Three quarts and a quarter more.
> These you pour into the punch bowl,
> Don't get any on the floor!"

Of course, the witch knew how to liquefy money. In the wink of an eye, the three and one quarter quarts were glistening in the giant bowl of Cold Fire. A golden glow enveloped the room.

Preposteror poured in the hellish liquid from his

shaker, and the potion shone no more. The brew was now as black as night, but here and there flashes of lightning like pulsating arteries shot through it and disappeared just as quickly.

The third instruction read:

> Time for shedding crocodile tears now,
> At a most alarming rate.
> Drop by drop you let them flow,
> Whilst bemoaning your sad state.
> After stirring up the briny
> Potion, mix in with the rest.
> Any wine that comes from whining
> Has to be the very best.

Now, of course, this was a little more difficult, for as has already been mentioned, evil sorcerers and witches cannot shed tears—not even false ones. But once again Preposteror rose to the occasion.

He remembered having stored away in his cellar several bottles of crocodile tears of a particularly bounteous vintage. They had been given him years and years ago by a certain head of state, who was one of Preposteror's most important clients. He brought up the bottles—there were seven of them—and after he had poured their contents into the black brew and stirred vigorously, the liquid changed color again and slowly turned red as blood.

And so it went, on and on. Sometimes Preposteror knew what to do and other times Tyrannia did. Propelled by their common evil will, they worked together as effortlessly as if they had never in their lives done anything else.

Only once did they share a bone of contention; namely, when they came to the part which read as follows:

> Take a scoop of fresh brain jelly
> (Good for building up your strength!)
> Corresponding most precisely
> To half your favorite color's length.

Of course, they both knew perfectly well *how* to measure the length of a color; that was not the problem. Their quarrel concerned *whose* favorite color should be used. Tyrannia insisted that it must be hers, because the instruction was written on that part of the scroll which belonged to her. Preposteror, on the other hand, maintained that it could only be his favorite color, since the entire experiment was taking place in his laboratory. They probably wouldn't have reached an agreement on this point so soon if they hadn't discovered, to their common relief, that half the length of sulphurous yellow was precisely as long as half the length of bilious green. Thus was the problem solved.

Now, surely nobody will honestly expect to find the entire list of ingredients necessary for the preparation of the Satanarchaeolidealcohellish Notion Potion printed here. The reason for their absence lies not only in the fact that such a complete list would unduly stretch out this story (after all, the scroll was about five yards long), but rather more in a well-founded worry: one can never know into whose hands a book such as this might fall, and no one should be tempted to undertake the brewing of this diabolic drink himself. There are already too many people of Preposteror's and Tyrannia's ilk in the world. Therefore, the sensible reader is kindly requested to accept the fact that most of the information must be withheld here.

Jacob Scribble and Morris sat at the foot of the cathedral, the steeple of which rose up like the face of a giant, jagged mountain into the nighttime sky. Both had their heads tilted back as far as they would go and gazed silently up into the air.

After a while the raven cleared his throat. "A barn owl acquaintance of mine used to live up there," he said. "Her name was Nun Bubu. A nice old lady. She had some crazy notions about life; that's why she preferred living all alone and went out only at night. But she sure knew a lot of things. If only she was there now, we could ask for advice."

"Where is she?" asked the cat.

"No idea. She emigrated because she couldn't stand the smog any longer. She always was a little finicky. Maybe she's long since died."

"What a shame," said Morris. And after a while he added, "Perhaps the cathedral bells bothered her as well. It must be awfully loud up there, so close to them."

"I don't really think so," said Jacob. "No owl was never bothered by cathedral bells."

And then he repeated once more, pensively, "The cathedral bells . . . wait a minute . . . cathedral bells . . ."

Suddenly he hopped into the air and screeched at the top of his lungs, "That's it! I've goooot it!"

"What?" asked a frightened Morris.

"Nothin'," answered Jacob, both feet back on the ground, and buried his head beneath his wing. "It won't work. No use. A lot of baloney. Forget it."

"What? Tell me!"

"Well, I was just thinking we could simply ring the New Year's bells a little earlier, like now, you understand? That would cancel out the reverse effect of the magic punch. They said themselves that even the first tiny tinkling of the New Year's bells would be enough. Don't you remember? Then nothing but good would come of their lying wishes, is what I thought."

The little cat stared at the raven. It took him a while to understand, but then his eyes began to glow. "Jacob," he said reverently, "Jacob Scribble, old friend, I think you are truly a genius. That is our salvation! Yes, I can really get excited about that."

"It would be nice," croaked Jacob peevishly, "but there's no way."

"Why not?"

"Well, who do you think is going to ring the bells?"

"Who? Why, you, of course! You simply fly up to the steeple now and ring them. Child's play."

"That's what you think!" croaked the raven. "Child's play, he says! Maybe for giant children. Have you ever seen church bells up close, my fuzzy feline?"

"No."

"That's what I thought! Because they're as big and heavy as a truck. You don't think that a raven can swing a truck, do you, especially one with rawmatism?"

"Aren't there smaller bells as well? Any bell would do."

"Listen, Morris. Even the smallest one is still as heavy as a wine barrel."

"Then we'll just have to try it together, Jacob. We're bound to succeed together. Come on! What are you waiting for?"

"Where do you think you're going, you crazy cat?"

"We must get into the steeple, where the bell ropes are. If we both pull on them with all our might, it is sure to work."

Inflamed by his enthusiasm for great deeds, Morris ran off in search of an entrance to the interior of the cathedral steeple. Jacob fluttered behind him, cursing and swearing all the while, and tried to make him understand that nowadays the bells are no longer rung anywhere by hand with ropes, but rather with electric motors by the push of a button.

"So much the better," said Morris. "Then all we have to do is find the button."

Yet this hope proved futile. The only door leading into the cathedral was locked. The little cat hung on to the great iron door handle and pulled—in vain!

"There you go, what did I tell you?" said the raven. "Give it up, kitty. No way means no way."

"There is a way!" said Morris, fierce with determination. He looked up the side of the cathedral. "If we can't go in, we'll go up."

"What's that supposed to mean?" screeched Jacob in horror. "You're not thinking of climbing up this cathedral from the outside, are you? With this wind? You must be off your rocker!"

"Do you have a better idea?" asked Morris.

"I know one thing," answered the raven, "that's the craziest, plucking thing I ever heard. And don't you think for a minute that I'm going to go along with it."

"Then I'll have to do it alone," said Morris.

The huge bowl of Cold Fire had meanwhile been filled to the brim. The liquid it contained was now of a violet hue. Although it was a mixture of the most bizarre ingredients, it was still far from being a Notion Potion. For this to occur, it first had to be magicalized; in other words, it had to go through an entire series of processes which would render it capable of receiving the true, dark powers of magic within its bosom.

This was the more scientific part of the undertaking and, as such, was Beelzebub Preposteror's department. His money-witching auntie could hand him what he needed, but that was about it.

The text they were dealing with was written in the technical language of lab sorcerers, and even Tyrannia could barely make head or tail of it. It read as follows:

Add some cathotymic flotion
To catafalcious polyglom,
Let it float in circular motion
In a dramolized an-atom.
Filter shlemielized ectoplasm
Into schizothalmic myrrh.
Burps of antigaseous spasms
Rise in alco-hymns and -hers.
Well-azipherized snorkels
Freeze to cheese in thermostations,
Chemically based on human morels
Of unflaxen proclamations.
Hapless, hopeless malt debates
If it passed the litmus test,
Whilst the sclerosis inflates
At a hundred-proof behest;

If the dose be not too spunky
From defective criminoil,
Then the complex remains flunky,
As unstable alcohoil.
And so if the brain should bubble
From this diabolic mix,
Chimera saws can nip the trouble
In the bud of sado-tricks.
This achieved, there builds a varnish
Of galaxyparallaxywax,
Which should alchemically tarnish
All asdrubal to the minimax.

And it went on like that for quite a while.

Preposteror had switched on all his magic computers, which were linked up to the hellish computer center, which was feeding them the necessary data. They were running at full steam—if one may speak of electronic machines in such terms—chirping, squeaking, rattling, flickering, and spitting out formulas and diagrams which told the sorcerer what to do next with the liquid in the bowl.

At one point, for example, he had to construct an antigravity field in order to achieve total weightlessness. In this way, he was able to lift the entire brew out of its container. The liquid floated in the center of the room like a big, slightly wobbly ball, and Preposteror was thus able to shoot it full of perversion particles, which would not have penetrated the bowl of Cold Fire.

However, he and his aunt were also afflicted by weightlessness during this phase, which made their work considerably more difficult. He was floating upside down under the ceiling of the laboratory while Tyrannia rotated horizontally on her own axis through the air. Still, he managed to turn off the antigravity generator with a lucky shot—which sent the ball of liquid splashing back into its container. Auntie Tye and he, however, crashed painfully back down to the floor.

But such occurrences are almost unavoidable with so risky an experiment and hardly dampened their fiery ardor.

Yet, shortly thereafter, an unforeseeable incident took place which was pretty frightening, even for the sorcerer and the witch; the liquid in the bowl suddenly came *alive*.

There exist one-celled creatures called amoebas, which are normally so tiny that they can be seen only under a microscope. In this case, however, the entire contents of the tureen metamorphosed into a single, giant amoeba, which left its container and crawled across the floor of the laboratory in one big, gelatinous puddle. The aunt and her nephew retreated before it and ultimately fled in different directions. At which point the giant cell split in two, one part slithering after each of them with the apparent intent of gobbling them up. Only with cunning and great effort were the sorcerer and the witch able to entice the two parts back into the bowl, where they immediately attacked one another in

a frenzy of hunger and ate each other up. Then they were merely liquid again and the danger was over.

At last the process of magicalization was finished. The substance in the container looked as shiny and opaque as mercury. It was now ready to receive each and every magic power; in this case, the secret power of making all wishes come true.

Morris had jumped onto a low canopy above the side entrance, from there onto the larger canopy above the main portal, and then scrambled onto a pointy little tower full of stone knobs, from the tip of which he executed a daring leap onto a ledge. He came within a hair of slipping off, for it was covered with snow and ice, yet he just about managed to keep his balance.

The raven fluttered up to him. "That's enough!" he said hoarsely. "Come down from there right now, do you hear me! You'll break every bone in your body. You're much too fat and out of shape for this sort of thing."

But the cat climbed on.

"Caw!" screamed Jacob furiously. "I could tear out my last feathers for not keeping my beak shut. Don't you have even an ounce of brains in that stupid cat's head of yours? I'm telling you there's no point. Those bells up there are much too heavy even for the two of us together."

"We'll see about that" was the little cat's undeterred reply.

He climbed on and on. The higher he got, the more relentlessly the storm raged about him.

He had already passed the large rose window above the main portal when he felt his strength suddenly draining away. Everything was turning in his head. He hadn't been in particularly good shape to begin with, but now his sojourn in the toxic-waste barrel was also beginning to make itself felt.

When he jumped over to a gargoyle portraying a grinning, pointy-eared devil, he started slipping slowly but surely. He would most certainly have fallen to the depths below—deadly even for an experienced cat—if Jacob hadn't come fluttering over and grabbed him by the tail at the last minute.

Panting and shivering, the little cat pressed against the wall to shield himself from the icy wind and tried to warm his numbed paws.

The raven perched in front of him.

"All right!" he said. "Now, all kidding aside. Even if you manage to get all the way up to the bells—and you never ever will—there's still no point. Why don't you use your brains for once in your life, pal! Let's just suppose that we really did manage to ring the bells—which, as I already said, is completely impossible—then your Maestro and my madam would naturally hear them as well. And if they hear them, then they're going to know right away that the reverse effect of their hooch has been canceled. So what? They can easily do without that now. The only reason they needed it was to fool us. But if we're not longer around, then there's no need for a reverse effect, is there? Then they can make evil wishes to their heart's content, which can literally come true. They don't have to watch their step because we're not there to bother them anymore. Or did you imagine you could climb all the way down the cathedral, run all the way back, and still be in time for the party later on? What were you thinking of, anyway? Do you know how you're going to end up? 'End' is the word indeed! You're going to come to a miserable end—and for nothing and for no good reason. And that will be the end of it."

But Morris wasn't listening. The raven's voice somehow made its way to his ears as from a great distance, but he felt much too sick and exhausted to follow such complicated trains of thought. He knew only one thing: it was just as far to the top now as it was to the bottom, and he wanted to go to the top because he had set his mind on it—whether it made sense or not. His whiskers were frosted over with ice and the bracing wind brought tears to his eyes, but he continued climbing.

"Hey!" the raven called bitterly after him. "I'll tell you one thing, *I'm* not helping you anymore from now on. If you want to kill yourself, then do it alone. I've got no use for heroes, I've got rawmatism, and I'm fed up with your stubbornness, just so that you know. I'm getting out of here, do you hear me. I'm beating it. I'm already gone! Toodle-oo! Aloha! Farewell! Adieu, comrade!"

At that very moment he saw that the little cat was swinging in the air, clinging to a gutter by only his front paws. He fluttered up, fought his way over to him through the stormy wind, grabbed him by the scruff of the neck with his beak, and pulled and tugged him into the gutter with his last ounce of strength.

"Well, I'll be stuffed!" he gasped. "I must have fallen out of the nest as an egg and landed on my head, no doubt about it."

Now he as well could feel his strength draining away. The poisonous contents of the barrel had also affected him. He felt as sick as a dog.

"I'm not budging from here," he snapped. "I'm staying put, I am. The world can come to an end as far as I care. I've had it. If I try to fly one more time, I'll go down like a stone."

He peered over the edge of the gutter. Way down below glittered the lights of the town.

Tyrannia took over the next phase of the operation—since the instructions stating how to force the power of wish fulfillment into the potion were written in gibberwitch. This is a Mix-Up Language which, in spite of the fact that it consists of our normal vocabulary, makes use of it in a completely topsy-turvy way. None of the words mean what they usually mean. *Globe*, for example, means *boy, barrel* means *girl, bursting at the seams* means *taking a walk, suitcase* means *garden, plucking* means *seeing, gulp* means *dog, swift* means *colorful, bluntly* means *suddenly.* Therefore, the sentence "A boy and a girl were taking a walk in the garden when they suddenly saw a colorful dog" would read thus in gibberwitch: "A globe and a barrel were bursting at the seams in a suitcase, when they bluntly plucked a swift gulp."

Tyrannia was fluent in gibberwitch. Without her knowledge the text of the formula made no sense what-

soever and no outsider would have interpreted it as anything other than sheer madness:

If you're the boss,
Take hobgoblin floss,
Spun from three fairies so hostile;
Puff in a glass
The billowing gas
Through two ecstatical nostrils!

If lumps are pumped
In humps and in clumps,
While they be crumpled in plaster,
Puddles will fall
Like oats from a stall
Onto the tie of the master.

If corks are torqued
By porky forks
In troubly twilight quagmires,
Then pickles stick
To nickels thick
With ticking ticker-tape wires.

If boring actors
With green benefactors
Should wash down their dumplings with rye,
Then foreign dishes
More dish than delicious
Set off the alarm in your thigh.

The entire passage was nearly five times as long, but this sample will have to suffice here.

After Tyrannia had translated everything, all the lights in the laboratory were turned off. Aunt and nephew stood in complete darkness and started conjuring for all they were worth. Apparitions emerged pell-mell from the darkness, shoved each other aside, and disappeared again as if in a feverish delirium.

Whirlwinds of fire formed in the air, turning and hissing and piling up into a kind of wind spout, which shrank and shrank until it reached the size of a little worm and was snapped up by a beak without a bird; a gray cloud floated in, with the skeleton of a dog hanging out of it by the tail; the skeleton bones changed into glowing snakes, entwined themselves like a ball of wool, and rolled across the floor; a horse's head with empty eye sockets bared its teeth and whinnied a frightful laugh; rats with tiny human faces danced ring-around-the-rosy around the bowl; a gigantic blue bedbug ridden by the witch had a kind of race with a big yellow scorpion of the same size, upon which crouched the sorcerer; a myriad of rosy-red leeches dripped from the ceiling; a black egg as tall as a man burst open, releasing many small black hands, which hopped about like spiders; an hourglass appeared, in which the grains of sand trickled from bottom to top; a burning fish swam around in the darkness; a tiny robot on a tricycle drove his lance into a stone pigeon, which then disintegrated into ashes; a giant, bald-headed character with a bare chest squeezed himself together like an accordion . . .

The Night of Wishes

And so it went on, the apparitions coming faster and faster and all disappearing eventually into the giant bowl, its liquid bubbling and hissing every time as if a red-hot iron rod had been thrust into it.

After one final raging whirlwind of indistinguishable images, the whole affair ended with a kind of explosion, which lit up the Notion Potion orange-red in its bowl of Cold Fire. Preposteror turned the lights back on.

He and his aunt were completely exhausted at first after their shared exertions. They had to perk themselves up by taking special magic power pills just to make it through the last and most difficult part of the preparation. But they could not allow themselves a rest now, for time was marching mercilessly on.

There was absolutely no way of carrying out this fourth and last part of the procedure in our world, within that which we call time and space. It was necessary to enter the Fourth Dimension. And that is why even the instructions were written in the Exorbitanian language, which there is positively no possibility of translating, since it expresses exclusively things and processes of the Fourth Dimension, which do not exist in our world.

This last and greatest effort was imperative in order to provide the potion with the reverse effect, which caused the opposite of all the wishes that one made to come true.

The instructions read as follows:

Hackamordax furycrass,
Zuckez crackabula:
Weirdafitz drac hornahiss
Liezabum paloola!
Piesypoisy shrillercry
Spitsnok angerufus.
Flopanorgy killereye
Badskin, crax o'lufus.
Ragemon us flackatass,
Crunchor, me molarens,
Gruselfoam sogrimmy grass—
Lookaboo zooharems.
Gurgoil choke ta bellyburst
Puckaduck spitootin,
Crankacralla scritchascratch
Blossomo—zashootin!
Nutwhat gulp Drambarrelous?
Hick gigantomula:
Hackamordax furycrass,
Liezabum paloola!

At first neither Preposteror nor Tyrannia could decipher this part of the formula. But they knew that one can speak and understand Exorbitanian only in the Fourth Dimension and so they had no choice but to enter therein without wasting another minute.

Now, the Fourth Dimension is not somewhere else, far away, but rather, right here where we are—we just can't perceive it, because neither our eyes nor our ears are properly equipped.

Aunt Tye herself would not have known what to do, but Beelzebub Preposteror knew a method of jumping from one dimension into another.

He went and got a syringe and a small strangely shaped bottle wherein sloshed a colorless liquid. It was labeled:

> Lucifer's
> Somersault
> Dimensionale

"You have to inject it directly into the blood," he explained.

Tyrannia nodded appreciatively. "I can see that I didn't send you to college in vain, after all, Bubby. Do you have any experience with the stuff?"

"A little, Tye. I've taken a little trip now and then, partly for experimental purposes, partly for pleasure."

"Then let's leave at once."

"However, I feel I must point out to you, dearest

Auntie, that this is not without an element of danger. It all depends on taking the right dose."

"What's that supposed to mean?"

Preposteror smiled at Tyrannia in a way which left her feeling not the least bit comfortable. "It means that you might land whoknowswhere, Tye-Tye," he said. "If the dose is just the tiniest bit too small, you fall down into the Second Dimension. Once there, you would be completely flat, as flat as a film projection. You wouldn't even have a backside, that's how flat you'd be. And most important of all, you would never be able to ascend into our accustomed Third Dimension on your own. It's possible that you would have to remain a two-dimensional screen image forever and ever, my poor old girl. If, however, the dose is too large, you are catapulted into the Fifth or the Sixth Dimension. Those upper dimensions are so confusing that you wouldn't even know which parts belonged to you and which ones didn't. It's possible that you would return with a few parts missing, or falsely assembled—if at all."

They stared at each other in silence for a few moments.

Tyrannia knew that her nephew was desperately in need of her help for the time being. As long as they hadn't finished brewing the Satanarchaeolidealcohellish Notion Potion, he could by no means do without her. And he knew that she knew it.

Now it was her turn to smile portentously. "Good," she said slowly. "I expect you'll do everything one hundred percent right. I'm relying fully on your egotism, Bubby."

He drew the colorless liquid into the syringe and both rolled up their left sleeves; he checked the dose carefully and gave first her, then himself, the injection.

Their silhouettes started vibrating, blurring, and being pulled and stretched grotesquely out of shape, until they were no longer to be seen.

In the bowl of Cold Fire, however, the strangest things started happening, seemingly of their own accord . . .

"Now I'm supposed to play the good guy?" the raven cackled to himself. "Yes, indeed—some good guy! I could tear myself to pieces for having such a goody-good idea. I'll never have another idea again, or else I'll spend the rest of my days a pedestrian, so help me. Ideas are nothing but trouble; trouble is all they bring."

But the cat didn't hear him, for he had already climbed

quite a bit farther, to the point where the sloped roof of the steeple began.

"He's really going to make it!" Jacob muttered. "Well, I'll be tarred and feathered, the guy's going to make it."

He gathered his last bit of strength and fluttered after the cat, but he couldn't find him in the dark. He landed on the head of a stone angel, who was trumpeting the arrival of Judgment Day, and searched all over.

"Morris, where are you?" he screamed.

No reply.

He screeched desperately into the black night, "Even if you really do make it all the way up to the bells, you mini-knight, you, and even if the two of us really do manage to ring them . . . which we won't . . . it's still pointless . . . because . . . if we ring them *now*, then it won't be the New Year's bells but just any old sound. The bells aren't the important thing; the important thing is that it must be the first stroke of twelve."

Not a sound was to be heard except for the crying of the wind, which blew around the corners of the steeple and the stone figures. Jacob gripped the head of the trumpeting angel and screamed in panic, "Hey, kitty, you still around, or have you already fallen down with the other snowflakes?"

For a fraction of a second he imagined he had heard a weak, pitiful meowing somewhere up above. He lunged into the darkness and flapped in the direction of the sounds, turning a few cartwheels on the way.

Although he no longer knew how, Morris had in fact managed to reach a lancet window, through which he was able to enter the steeple. The last of his strength finally ebbed the moment Jacob landed beside him. The

little cat fainted and tumbled down into the steeple, though luckily not too far. There he lay in the all-enveloping darkness, a tiny bundle of fur on the wooden beams of the belfry.

Jacob hopped down to him and nudged him with his beak. But Morris didn't budge.

"Morris," croaked the raven, "are you dead?"

When he got no reply, he lowered his head slowly. A tremor shook his body.

"I've got to hand it to you, kitty," he said quietly and solemnly, "you may not have had an awful lot of brains, but you were still a hero, somehow. Your fancy ancestors would have been pretty proud of you, if they had ever existed."

Then everything went black before his eyes and he fell over. The wind whistled around the tip of the steeple and blew in snow, which gradually covered the two animals.

Just above them, the mighty bells hung huge and shadowy from the rafters black with age, waiting silently for the beginning of the New Year, which they were to herald with their powerful voices.

The potion whirled around in its bowl of Cold Fire at a terrifying speed, matching that of a centrifuge, for the tail of a comet, glistening and showering sparks, was circling within it like a giant goldfish run amok.

Meanwhile, Preposteror and Tyrannia had returned from the Fourth Dimension and were sprawled out on their chairs, completely exhausted. They would have loved to really let themselves go for a few minutes, just to unwind, but that was precisely what they could by no means permit themselves to do—it would have placed them in utmost jeopardy.

They stared glassy-eyed at the bowl.

Although the potion was basically finished and they didn't have anything else to do, there was one more difficulty to overcome, possibly the greatest of all, in these remaining minutes before the completion of their devilish work. It consisted of *not* doing a certain something.

The Night of Wishes

According to the very last instruction on the parchment scroll, they now needed only wait until the liquid had completely settled and all the sediment dissolved without leaving a trace. But until that moment they were not allowed *to ask a single question*, let alone as much as *think* one.

Every question (for example, "Will it work?" or "Why am I doing this?" or "What's the point?" or "What is going to come of this?") contains an element of doubt. And you were absolutely forbidden to doubt anything in these final moments. You were even forbidden to ask yourself in your thoughts why you were forbidden to ask any questions.

Because as long as the potion had not completely settled and become clear and transparent, it was in a highly sensitive and unstable state, which made it react even to thoughts and feelings. As much as the slightest doubt in its powers could make the entire brew explode like an atomic bomb and blow up not only the sorcerer and the witch but also the Villa Nightmare; yes, even the entire neighborhood.

Now, it is well known that nothing is more difficult than *not* thinking of a certain something you have been told. You don't normally think of kangaroos, for example. But if you are forbidden to think about kangaroos for the next five minutes, how can you avoid thinking of just those kangaroos? There is only one way: you have to concentrate on something else, whatever it may be, with all your might.

And so Preposteror and Tyrannia sat there, their eyes

Michael Ende

literally popping from the fear and exertion of not thinking any questions.

The sorcerer was reciting quietly all the poems he had
learned in his kinderdesert days (kinder*desert* being for
evil sorcerers what kinder*garten* is for normal people).

He muttered in a breathless monotone:

"I am a little monster swine
and stink and snort and snigger.
I want to be a little pain
until I get much bigger."

and:

"The little boy couldn't stop grinning
When he bit off the pollywog's head,
'Cause he knew very well that sinning
Is more fun than praying in bed."

and:

"Goldilocks loves gently yanking
The legs from the bodies of bees,
For she knows that she could earn a spanking
By sparing the buggers their knees."

And even the lullaby his mother used to sing to him
when he was just a little baby:

"Rock-a-bye-baby!
Your dad's in the navy.
He sails through the night
Sucking blood left and right.
Rock-a-bye-baby!

"Drink-a-bye-baby!
Your fangs grow like crazy.
Papa taught you right:
Here a bite, there a bite!
Drink-a-bye-baby!"

and other uplifting rhymes and songs.

Meanwhile, Tyrannia Vampirella was calculating in her head how much a single crown deposited in a savings account at 6 percent interest in the year zero would have accumulated in combined interest up to the present day—assuming, of course, that the bank still existed.

In doing so she used the formula known to all money sorcerers and witches:

$$Kn = Ko(1 + i)\eta$$

She had already arrived at a sum of money corresponding in value to several gold balls the size of the earth, although she had still not reached the present day. She calculated and calculated, because she was calculating for her life.

But the longer the minutes stretched—the potion had

still not completely settled and cleared—the more Preposteror had the feeling that his whole, long body was bending into the shape of a question mark. And it appeared to Tyrannia that all the endless columns of figures before her eyes consisted of myriads of microscopically small question marks, which swarmed about and refused to be lined up in neat little rows.

"By all the cloned genes!" Preposteror sighed at last. "I can't go on much longer. I don't know any more poems . . ."

And Tyrannia whispered fearfully, "I got my calculations mixed up. Soon . . . soon . . . I'm going to think of . . ."

Whack!

In decisive desperation, the nephew had dealt his aunt a mighty slap in the face.

"Ouch!" cried the witch furiously. "You just wait!"

And with that she gave her nephew such a wallop that his glasses went flying right across the laboratory.

An exchange of blows ensued which would have done the toughest of boxers proud.

When they finally stopped, they found themselves sitting on the floor, staring at each other breathlessly. The nephew had a black eye and his aunt a bloody nose.

"Nothing personal, Tye," said Preposteror. Then he pointed at the bowl of Cold Fire.

"Look!"

In the meantime, the tail of the comet had stopped swishing and sparkling, all the sediment had disap-

peared, and the Satanarchaeolidealcohellish Notion Potion shone still and clear in all the colors of the rainbow.

Both of them uttered a deep sigh of relief.

"That slap was our salvation," said Tyrannia. "You are a good boy, after all, Bubby."

"You know what, Auntie," said Preposteror, "now that the danger is over, we can think whatever we want. And we should do just that to our hearts' content, don't you think?"

"I do, indeed," said the witch, rolling her eyes with relish.

Preposteror smirked. Of course, he had something up his sleeve. Auntie had a surprise coming.

As the raven and the little cat slowly regained consciousness, they at first thought they were dreaming. The icy wind had settled down, everything was quiet, the stars sparkled in the nighttime sky, they were no longer cold, and the huge belfry was illuminated by a wonderful golden glow. One of the big stone figures, which had been gazing down upon the town from outside the lancet windows for centuries, had turned around and come in. But the statue no longer had a stony appearance; it looked very much alive.

The figure in question was a delicate old man in a

long coat of gold brocade, the shoulders of which were heaped with snow. He wore a miter on his head and carried a shepherd's crook in his left hand. His watery blue eyes gazed at the two animals from under bushy white eyebrows in a curious but not unfriendly manner.

One could have taken him for Saint Nicholas at first sight, but this could not be, for no beard adorned his chin. And who had ever heard of a clean-shaven Saint Nick?

The old gentleman raised his right hand, and Jacob and Morris suddenly realized that they could neither move nor utter the tiniest sound. They were both afraid, yet at the same time, they somehow felt safe.

"Well, you two scamps," said the old gentleman, "what are you doing up here?"

He came a little closer and bent over them in order to get a closer look. He squinted a bit—apparently he was nearsighted.

The raven and the cat sat there and looked at him.

"I know what you're up to," the old gentleman said. "You shouted it loud enough while you were bouncing up here. You want to swipe my beautiful New Year's chime. To tell you the truth, I don't think that's very nice. I've got nothing against a good joke, after all I'm Father New Year, but what you two were up to is a bad joke, don't you think? Well, in any case, I got here just in the nick of time."

The two animals tried to protest, but they still could not speak.

"I guess you didn't know," said Father New Year, "that I come here for a few minutes every year on this occasion to make sure everything is all right. Perhaps I should turn you into stone figures for a while and stick you between these pillars in return for the dumb joke you wanted to play on me. Yes, I guess that's what I'll do. At least until tomorrow morning, so that you can have time to think about your actions. But first I want to hear what you have to say for yourselves."

But the animals sat motionless.

"Have you suddenly forgotten how to speak?" asked Father New Year in astonishment. Then he remembered. "Oh yes, of course, excuse me, I had completely forgotten . . ."

He raised his hand once again. "You can speak now, but one after the other, and no cheap excuses, if you please."

And so our two misunderstood heroes were finally able to croak and meow their explanations of what had driven them up here and who they were and what the evil plans of the sorcerer and the witch consisted of. In their eagerness, they sometimes spoke simultaneously, which made it all the more difficult for Father New Year to get the whole story. But the longer he listened, the friendlier was the gleam in his eyes.

Meanwhile, Beelzebub Preposteror and Tyrannia Vampirella had maneuvered themselves into a deadlocked situation.

The sorcerer had had an insidious plan when he suggested that they give free rein to their thoughts in order to relax a little. He wanted to trick his unsuspecting aunt. The Notion Potion was ready and so he no longer needed her assistance. He had decided to cut her out, so as to have the unimaginable power of the magic brew all to himself. But of course, Tyrannia had only pretended to agree to a little break, for precisely the same reason: she also thought that the time had come to finally get rid of her nephew.

They both gathered all their magic powers once more at the same moment and attempted to paralyze each other with their magic gazes. They sat opposite one another and stared into each other's eyes. A terrible, silent battle raged between them. But it soon became clear that they were a perfect match as far as willpower was concerned. And so they sat, without exchanging a word and without moving a muscle—and the sweat ran down their faces from sheer exhaustion. Neither one let the other out of his sight; they both hypnotized and hypnotized for all they were worth.

A fat fly, who had decided to spend the winter somewhere on one of the dusty shelves, suddenly woke up and buzzed around the laboratory. It felt something attracting it, as would a strong ray of light. Yet it was not light but rather the paralyzing power rays from the eyes of the witch and the sorcerer, flashing back and

forth between them like powerful electrical discharges. The fly got caught in the middle and fell immediately to the floor with a soft plop, unable to so much as move a leg. And so it remained for the rest of its short life.

Meanwhile, the aunt and her nephew were also unable to move. They had each been hypnotized themselves right when they were most enjoying hypnotizing each other. And naturally, for that very reason, they could no longer stop hypnotizing one another.

By and by it dawned on them both that they had made a fatal error, but now it was too late. They were neither of them capable of moving so much as a finger, let alone turning their heads in another direction or closing their eyes in order to interrupt the magic gaze. Neither of them could do that *anyway*, at least not until the other did the same, or else they would have been helplessly at the mercy of the other's power. The witch couldn't stop before the sorcerer stopped, and the sorcerer couldn't stop before the witch stopped. They had got themselves into something which, in conjuring circles, is known as a *circulus vitiosus*, that is to say, a vicious circle—and one of their own making at that.

"You never stop learning," said Father New Year. "Just goes to show how even I can still make mistakes. I did you an injustice, my little friends, and I beg your forgiveness."

"Don't mention it, Monsignore," said Morris with an elegant wave of his paw. "That kind of thing can happen even in the best circles."

And Jacob added, "Forget it, Reverend Father, nothing to get worked up about. I'm used to being treated badly."

Father New Year grinned, but then became serious again. "What are we going to do now?" he asked, a bit helplessly. "What you've just told me sounds truly awful."

Filled with renewed heroic enthusiasm at such unexpected, and prominent, assistance, Morris suggested, "If Monsignore would be so kind as to ring the bells himself . . ."

But Father New Year shook his head. "No, no, my little ones, that is not the way! It doesn't work like that at all. Everything in the world must have its proper place, time, and space: the end of the old year as well as the beginning of the new. One can't just change things willfully or else everything will go topsy-turvy . . ."

"What did I tell you?" said the woebegone raven. "Nothing doing! It was all for the birds. Everything in its place, even if the entire world goes to the devil."

Father New Year didn't hear Jacob's unseemly remark; he appeared to be lost in thought. "Yes, yes. Evil, I remember," he sighed. "What is Evil, anyway, and why does it have to exist? We have occasional debates on the subject up yonder, but it is truly a great mystery, even for the likes of us."

His eyes took on a vacant look. "You know, my little friends, Evil appears quite different when seen from the point of view of eternity than when seen from within the kingdom of time. Up yonder one sees that it actually always serves Good in the long run. It is, so to speak, a contradiction in itself. It is constantly striving for power over Good, but without Good it could not exist—and if it ever achieved total power, it would have to destroy precisely that over which it desires to wield said power. That's why it can last only as long as it is incomplete, my dears. If it were complete, it would cancel itself out. That's why it has no place in eternity. Only Good is eternal, for it contains itself without contradiction—"

"Hey!" shouted Jacob Scribble, tugging vigorously

Michael Ende

on the golden coat with his beak. "No offense, Reverend
Blather—excuse me; Father, I mean—but that doesn't
matter a hill of beans at the moment, if you don't mind
my saying so. By the time you're done with your fillosophy, it'll be too late."

Father New Year was obviously having a difficult time
finding his way back to the present. "What?" he asked,
smiling dreamily. "What were we talking about?"

"We were saying," explained Morris, "that we absolutely must do something right away in order to prevent a terrible calamity, Monsignore."

"Oh yes, oh yes," said Father New Year, "but what?"

"Well, Monsignore, I guess only a miracle can save
us now. But you are a saint. Can't you just make a
miracle—a little, tiny one?"

"Just a miracle!" repeated Father New Year, slightly
flabbergasted. "My dear little friend, it's not as easy
making miracles as you think. None of us can make a
miracle unless he's received a commission from up
above. First of all, I'd have to put in an application at a
higher level, and it could take a long time before it gets
approved—if at all."

"How long?" asked Morris.

"Months, years, possibly decades," answered Father
New Year.

"That's too long!" croaked Jacob sullenly. "Then we
might as well forget it. We need something now, right
now."

Father New Year's eyes started glazing over again.
"Miracles," he said, his voice filled with awe, "do not

change the order of things; they are not magic; they are of a higher order inconceivable to the limited, earthly mind . . ."

"That may be," rasped Jacob Scribble, "but unfortunately, *we* are dealing with magic, and we're dealing with it tonight."

"Yes, yes," said Father New Year, who once again was having difficulty descending from his higher spheres of thought. "To tell you the truth, my little friends, I understand your sitution, but I'm afraid there isn't all that much I can do for you. Besides, I'm not at all sure that I'm allowed to act on my own authority in such cases. But since I happen to be here anyway, there just might be one little possibility . . ."

Morris nudged the raven and whispered. "He's going to help us."

"Let's wait and see," Jacob replied skeptically.

"If I understood you correctly a while ago," Father New Year said, "then one single chime of the New Year's bells would be enough to cancel out the reverse effect of the Archaeolinear . . ." He got stuck.

"Satanarchaeolidealcohellish Notion Potion," Morris interceded helpfully.

"Precisely," said Father New Year, "to cancel out the reverse effect of same. Wasn't that it?"

"That's the way we heard it," confirmed the cat, and the raven nodded in agreement.

"And you think that alone is going to be enough to stop this terrible thing?"

"Sure," said Jacob, "but only if those two devils don't get wind of what we're doing. They would wish Good in order to do Evil, but only Good would come of it."

"Well, let's see." Father New Year thought it over. "I guess I could spare you a single note from my New Year's concert. I only hope nobody will notice that it's missing."

"I'm sure they won't," Morris cried eagerly. "One tone more or less doesn't matter in a concert; any singer knows that."

"Couldn't it be a little more?" suggested Jacob. "I mean, just in case and to be on the safe side."

"Certainly not," said Father New Year sternly. "Actually, that's already too much, considering the order of things—"

"All right!" the raven interrupted hastily. "No harm in asking. But how is it supposed to work anyway, Reverend Father? If you ring the bell now, those two villains will hear it, too, and they'll be warned."

"Ring the bells now?" asked Father New Year, his eyes once more taking on a distant expression. "Ring the bells now? There would be no point, for they wouldn't be the New Year's bells. That can only happen at midnight, and so it must remain, because the beginning and the end . . ."

"Exactly!" rasped the raven grimly. "Because of the order of things. But then it'll be too late, it will."

Morris signaled him to be quiet.

Father New Year's gaze seemed to wander into the distance. He suddenly looked much bigger and most awesome.

"In eternity," he said, "we live beyond space and time. There is no before and no after, and cause and effect do not follow one another either, but form a permanent unity. That's why I can give you the note now, even though it won't sound until midnight. Its effect will precede its cause, as is the case with so many of eternity's gifts."

The animals looked at each other. Neither of them understood what Father New Year had just said. But he stroked the great curve of the largest bell slowly with gentle fingers, and suddenly he had a crystal-clear ice cube in his hand. He held it out to the animals between thumb and index finger, and they eyed it from all sides. A beautiful, heavenly light in the form of a single note glistened and sparkled within the crystal of ice.

"Here," he said kindly. "Take this, carry it back quickly, and drop it into the Hellishandsoonandsoforth

Potion without their noticing it. But mind your aim and don't lose it, for this is the only one you have and I can't give you another."

Jacob Scribble took the ice cube carefully in his beak and, since he could no longer speak, mumbled, "Hmm! Hmm! Hmm!" accompanying each sound with a bow.

Morris executed an elegant bow and scrape as well, and meowed, "Most humble thanks, Monsignore. We shall prove worthy of your trust. But could you possibly give us one more bit of advice? How are we going to get back there on time?"

Father New Year gazed at him and retrieved his thoughts once more from the distant, distant eternity. "What did you say, my little friend?" he asked, smiling as only saints can smile. "What were we talking about?"

"I beg your pardon," stuttered the little cat. "It's only, I don't think I'll be able to climb all the way back down the cathedral. And poor Jacob is also at the end of his feathers."

"Oh yes, of course," said Father New Year. "Well, I don't think that should be a problem. You will fly with the bell tone, so it will only take a few seconds to get there. Just be sure to hold one another tight. And now I really must bid you farewell. It was a great pleasure meeting two such brave and upright creatures of God. I shall tell of you up yonder."

He raised his hand in a gesture of benediction.

The cat and the raven clung to one another, and off

they flew through the night at the speed of sound. To their great surprise, they found themselves back in the cat's chamber only seconds later. The window was open and it was as if they had never left the little room.

But the ice cube with the beautiful light within it that Jacob Scribble held in his beak proved that it had not been a dream.

The lives of black magicians are so very strenuous and unpleasant because they must have all creatures, indeed even the simplest objects, within their sphere of influence constantly and completely under their control. They can never allow themselves a moment's negligence or weakness, for all their power relies on force. No creature, not even an object, would ever serve them willingly. That is why they must constantly enslave all and sundry around them by means of their magic aura. If they let up for even as much as a minute, they can expect a spontaneous rebellion.

It may be difficult for a normal person to comprehend

that there are people in this world who enjoy exercising this kind of force. And yet there always were, and today there still exist quite a few who would stop at nothing to acquire and maintain such power—and not only among sorcerers and witches.

The more willpower Preposteror used to counter Tyrannia's debilitating hypnotic spell with his own, the less energy he had left to keep the countless elemental spirits in his so-called natural history museum under permanent control.

It began when that particularly repulsive little creature, the book grump, began to stir, stretched and twisted, looked around as if upon waking, and, once it realized where it was, commenced romping about so wildly in its glass jar that the whole kit and caboodle tipped off the shelf. The book grump didn't fall far enough to sustain serious injuries, yet far enough for its glass prison to shatter.

As soon as the others, who were already thumping and gesticulating wildly, noticed this, they followed suit. One jar after another came crashing down, the liberated victims joining in to liberate the remaining prisoners, and so there were more and ever more of them. Soon the dark corridor was swarming with hundreds and hundreds of tiny figures—all manner and shape of gnomes and hobgoblins, water sprites, elves, salamanders, and trolls. They all milled and stumbled about, for they didn't know their way around the gloomy Villa Nightmare.

The book grump paid little attention to the others, since it was much too educated to believe in the existence of such beings. It flared its nostrils and sniffed the air. It hadn't had the chance to grump about a book for a terribly long time and was craving to do so. Its infallible nose told it where suitable material could be found and it headed off in the direction of the laboratory. A few gnomes followed it, haltingly at first, in the hope that it would lead them to freedom. Then more and more creatures joined the parade, until finally, a thousand-strong army was on the march, headed by the book grump, which had taken over the revolutionary leadership without really meaning to.

Now, all these spirits may be small in size, but their powers are great, as we all know. When this army stormed the laboratory and started smashing everything in sight, the walls shook all the way down to the foundations as if an earthquake were taking place. Window-panes shattered, doors burst open, and walls were rent asunder as if they had been hit by bombs.

Ultimately, the objects, which were still heavily charged all and sundry with Preposteror's magic powers, began coming eerily to life and defending themselves against the rebels. The bottles, test tubes, flasks, and crucibles started moving, whistling, puffing, ballet dancing, and spraying the essences they contained at their attackers. Many shattered during the battle, although quite a few elemental spirits were also taught a painful lesson and opted to flee to the safety of the Dead Park, limping and wailing all the while.

The book grump had retreated from this noisy rumpus into the stillness of the library, where it peacefully went about satisfying its need. It pulled out the first tome it could find and immediately started grumping to its heart's content. But the magic book would have none of this and snapped at it.

While they were still fighting, all the other books in the library started coming to life. Row upon row, they marched down from the shelves in their hundreds and their thousands.

Now, it is a well-known fact that books often hate each other's guts. Even with normal books, no one with any sensitivity would put *Justine*, of all books, next to *Heidi*, or *Revenue Law* next to *The Neverending Story*, although normal books cannot defend themselves, of course. But sorcerers' books are a different story, particularly when they have just shaken off the shackles of slavery. Within a short period of time, various platoons had formed among the countless books, according to their tables of contents—and they now charged one another with open, snarling covers and tried to gobble each other up. Even the book grump was seized with fear and fled.

In the end, even the furniture started joining in the common ruckus. Heavy wardrobes grunted into action, chests full of household articles and china hopped solemnly about, stools and armchairs whirled around on one leg like ice skaters, tables galloped and bucked like broncos at a rodeo—in short, 'twas a veritable witches' sabbath.

The clock with the cruel works had stopped hitting its own sore thumb with the hammer and was flailing wildly about. Its hands turned like propellers, and it flew from the wall and circled the battlefield like a helicopter. And every time it passed over the heads of the sorcerer and the witch, who still could not move, it hammered full force.

In the meantime, the last remaining elemental spirits had fled outside and scattered to the four winds. The books, furniture, and objects, which had, up to now, fought principally among themselves, increasingly directed their common rage against their oppressors. Preposteror and Tyrannia were hit by flying books, bitten by the stuffed shark, sprayed by glass flasks, elbowed by chests of drawers, and knocked over by bucking table legs, until they both rolled across the floor at the same time. But that, of course, broke the mutual hypnotic trance and the two of them were able to struggle to their feet.

"Stop!" thundered Preposteror in a powerful voice.

He raised his arms, and green-glowing thunderbolts shot out of all ten fingers into every corner of the laboratory, into all the other rooms of the Villa Nightmare, through the crooked corridors, up the stairs to the attic, and down to the cellar. At the same time he roared:

"Things and beings, flesh and plaster,
 Of my power do take heed!
 Once again your fate's decreed
 By the one and only Master."

He wasn't able to order back the elemental spirits, for they had already escaped the clutches of his magic influence, but the bedlam inside the villa instantly came to a stop. Whatever was buzzing through the air crashed or clattered to the floor; jaws were pried apart and limbs unwound. Everything lay still—except for the long parchment scroll bearing the formula, which was still coiling like a giant worm, since it had fallen into the fireplace and was burning to ashes.

Preposteror and Tyrannia gazed about the laboratory, puffing loudly. It was a dreadful sight: nothing but tattered books, broken windows and containers, upended and demolished furniture, shards of glass and china and rubble. Essences dripped from the walls and ceiling and formed smoking puddles on the floor. The sorcerer and the witch had not been roughed up any less; they were covered with bumps, scrapes, and black-and-blue marks, and their clothes were ragged and soiled.

Only the Satanarchaeolidealcohellish Notion Potion still stood intact in the middle of the room in its bowl of Cold Fire.

The cat and the raven returned to the cat's chamber from the steeple just in time to hear the shattering and bursting of the preserve jars in the corridor. Since they had no idea what the cause of this hellish racket was, they fled out into the dark garden and onto the branch of a dead tree. There they sat, pressed closely together, listening in horror to the supposed earthquake, which shook the entire villa, and watching the windowpanes burst.

"Do you think they are having a quarrel?" whispered Morris.

Jacob, who was still desperately holding the ice cube with the beautiful little light in his beak, could only mumble, "Hmm, hmm?" and shrug his wings.

Meanwhile, the wind had stopped blowing. The dark clouds had disappeared, and the starry night glittered like a million diamonds. But it had become colder still.

The two animals shivered and shifted closer together.

Preposteror and Tyrannia stood facing each other, the gigantic bowl between them. They stared at each other with unmasked hatred.

"You damned old witch," he growled, "this is all your fault."

"No, it's yours, you conniving swindler," she hissed. "Don't you ever do that again!"

"You started it."

"No, you did."

"You're a liar."

"You wanted to get rid of me and drink the potion all by yourself."

"That's exactly what you wanted to do."

There was an embittered silence.

"Bubby," the witch said at last, "let's be reasonable. No matter whose fault it was, we've already lost an

Michael Ende

awful lot of time. And if we don't want to have brewed the potion in vain, then it's high time to get down to business."

"You're right, Aunt Tye," Preposteror said with a crooked grin. "We should bring in the two spies without further delay, so we can finally start the party."

"I better go along with you," said Tyrannia, "otherwise you're likely to get some strange ideas in your head again, my boy."

And they climbed hastily over the rubble and rushed out into the corridor.

"They're gone now," whispered Morris, who had night sight and could better observe the interior of the house. "Quick now, Jacob! Fly ahead, I'll follow you."

Jacob fluttered unsteadily down from the branch to one of the broken laboratory windows. Morris, his paws numb with cold, first had to clamber down the dead tree, work his way through the high snow to the house, jump up onto the window ledge, and climb carefully through the hole in the pane. He noticed a few bloody feathers along the jagged edge of the hole and panicked.

"Jacob," he whispered, "what happened? Are you hurt?"

But then he sneezed a few times so hard that he almost fell over. No doubt about it, on top of everything else he had had the bad luck to catch a cold.

He looked around the laboratory and took in the devastation. "Good heavens," he felt like saying, "what a mess!"

But all that remained of his voice was a hoarse squeak.

Jacob was already sitting on the rim of the giant bowl, trying repeatedly to throw in the ice cube, but without success. His beak was frozen shut.

He cast a series of helpless glances in Morris's direction, and kept on saying, "Hmm! Hmm! Hmm!"

"Just listen!" exclaimed the little cat with a tragic squeak. "Do you hear my voice? That's all that is left of it. Gone forever!"

The raven hopped angrily along the rim of the bowl.

"What are you waiting for?" Morris squeaked. "Go ahead and throw in the note!"

"Hmm! Hmm!" said Jacob, frantically trying to open his beak.

"Wait, I'll help you," whispered Morris, who had finally understood. He jumped onto the rim of the bowl as well, but he was shivering so hard from head to toe that he came within a hairsbreadth of falling in. He barely managed to hang on to Jacob, who was having trouble keeping his balance himself.

Then they heard the voice of the witch coming from the corridor. "Not there? What do you mean, they're not there? Hellihello, Jacoboo, my little raven, where are you hiding?"

And then Preposteror's hoarse bass: "Mauricio di Mauro, my dear little kitty, come to your good Maestro!"

The voices came closer.

"Great Tom in Kitty Heaven, help us," Morris exclaimed, trying all the while to pry open Jacob's beak with his two paws.

There was a sudden plonk! The whole giant bowl began to vibrate, but there was not a sound—the surface of the liquid merely rippled as if it was getting goose bumps. Then it smoothed over again, and the ice cube

with the bell tone within it had dissolved in the Notion Potion without leaving a trace.

The two animals jumped down from the bowl and hid behind a tipped-over chest of drawers. At that very moment, Preposteror entered with Tyrannia in tow.

"What was that?" she asked suspiciously. "Something was here. I can feel it."

"How could anything have happened?" Preposteror said. "I'd just like to know where those animals are. If they have escaped, then we've gone to all the trouble of making the potion in vain."

"Now wait a minute," said the witch, "what do you mean in vain? After all, now we're guaranteed to fulfill our contractual obligations by midnight. What's wrong with that?"

Preposteror put his hand over her mouth. "Shush!" he hissed. "Are you crazy, Tye? Perhaps they're here somewhere listening to us."

They both pricked up their ears—and of course Morris had to choose just that moment for a wicked sneeze.

"Aha!" cried Preposteror. "Bless you, Virtuoso!"

The animals came out hesitatingly from behind the chest of drawers. Jacob, his breast feathers stained with blood, dragged along his wings and Morris tottered forward.

"Aha!" added Tyrannia with a drawl. "And how long have you been here, my little ones?"

"We just this second came in the window," croaked Jacob, "and I cut myself, as you can see, madam."

"And why didn't you stay in the cat's chamber as you were ordered?"

"We did," the raven said, winging it once again. "We were sleeping the whole time, but when it started bumping and crashing all of a sudden, we got so ascared that we fleed into the garden. What was going on here, anyway? That was absolutely terribulous. And just look at the two of you! Whatever happened to you?"

He nudged the cat, who echoed with a weak voice, ". . . happened to you?"

And then he was seized by a terrible coughing attack.

Whoever has seen a little cat in the throes of a coughing fit knows what a heartbreaking sight that can be. The sorcerer and the witch pretended to be very concerned.

"That sounds just awful, my little one," said Preposteror.

"I think you both look pretty beat," added Tyrannia. "Is that all that happened to you?"

"Is that all?" screeched Jacob. "Well, thanks a bunch! We were squatting up in that tree out there for half an hour because we were ascared to come back—and in lousy, cold weather like this. Is that all! I am a raven, madam, and no penguin! My rawmatism is acting up in every bone of my body, so that I can't move as much as a wing. Is that all! We both caught our deaths out there. Is that all! Aaah, I said it from the start, this will come to no good end."

"And in here?" asked Tyrannia with narrowed eyes. "Did you touch anything here?"

"Nothin' at all," rasped Jacob. "That tussle with the paper snake was enough for us."

"Let well enough alone, Tye," said the sorcerer. "We're only wasting time."

But she shook her head. "I'm sure I heard something."

She examined the animals with a piercing look.

Jacob opened his beak in reply, only to close it again. He had run out of stories.

"That was I," squeaked Morris. "I beg your pardon, but my tail was frozen as stiff as a walking stick, and completely numb to boot, and I accidentally bumped into that bowl with it—but only ever so lightly, and nothing happened, Maestro."

The raven cast an approving glance at his colleague.

The sorcerer and the witch seemed to be appeased.

"You may be wondering why this place looks like a

battlefield, my little friends," said Preposteror. "You'd no doubt like to know who manhandled me and my poor old auntie in such a fashion."

"Yes, who was it?" cackled Jacob.

"Well, I'll tell you," the sorcerer said in an unctuous tone of voice. "While you two were slumbering peacefully in that cozy cat's chamber, the two of us were fighting a terrible battle—a battle against enemy forces which wanted to destroy us. And do you know why?"

"No, why?" asked Jacob.

"Well, after all, we promised you a big and wonderful surprise, didn't we? And we keep our promises. Can you guess what it is?"

"No, what?" asked Jacob, with Morris murmuring in unison.

"Now hear ye well, my little friends, and be of good cheer," said Preposteror. "My dear aunt and I have worked indefatigably and at great personal sacrifice"—here he cast a sharp glance at Tyrannia—"at great personal sacrifice for the good of all living things. The power of money"—here he pointed to the witch—"and the power of knowledge"—here he laid his hand on his chest and lowered his gaze humbly—"shall now join together to bring happiness and prosperity to all suffering creatures and the whole of humanity."

He paused a moment to smooth his forehead with a theatrical flourish before continuing. "However, the road to destruction is often paved with good intentions. The powers of evil set upon us and did all they could to hinder our noble purpose—the result lies before your eyes. But they could not defeat us, for we two were as one, heart and soul. We put them to flight. And here you see our mutual creation: that marvelous drink which possesses the heavenly magic power of granting any and all wishes. It goes without saying that such great power can only be placed in the hands of personages far above using it for even the slightest egotistical motives, personages such as Aunt Tye and myself . . ."

Apparently, this was too much even for him to swallow. He had to hold his hand in front of his mouth to hide the wicked giggle erupting there.

Tyrannia gave him a nod and quickly took the floor. "You really put that very nicely, my dear boy. I am touched. The great moment has arrived."

Then she bent down to pet the animals and said in a significant tone of voice, "And you, my dear little ones, have been chosen to witness this fabulous event. It is a great honor for you and I'm sure you are just thrilled, aren't you?"

"And how!" croaked Jacob grimly. "Thanks a lot."

Morris wanted to say something as well, but had another coughing fit instead.

The sorcerer and the witch searched among the broken china, found two undamaged glasses and a ladle, pulled up two chairs, and sat down on opposite sides of the bowl.

They filled their glasses with the opalescent brew and emptied them in one gulp, without setting them down. When they were done, they both gasped for air, for the potion was alcohellishly strong indeed. Smoke rings puffed out of Preposteror's ears and Tyrannia's sparse wisps of hair rolled up into corkscrew curls.

"Aaah!" Preposteror said, wiping his mouth with the back of his hand. "I needed that."

"Indeed," Tyrannia said. "Most invigorating."

And then they began launching their wishes. Of course, these had to be rhymed in order for the magic to work.

The sorcerer was the quicker of the two with his first rhyme:

Michael Ende

"O potent bowl of omnipotent potion,
  Now hear my wish and grant me a notion:
  Ten thousand dying trees in the wood
  Shall again flourish and grow,
  While those that are healthy and still looking good
  Certainly shall remain so."

By now the witch was ready with her rhyme:

"O potent bowl of omnipotent potion,
  Now hear my wish and grant me a notion:
  Shares in the corporation Extinct, Inc.
  Shall no longer double and gain.
  They'll lie around useless and fester and stink
  Until they are flushed down the drain."

And then they poured themselves another glass and hastily tossed it down in one gulp, because they no longer had much time. After all, they had to have drunk every drop by midnight.

Once again Preposteror was quicker with his rhyme:

"O potent bowl of omnipotent potion,
  Now hear my wish and grant me a notion:
  The Thames, Mississippi, the Danube and Rhine,
  And each other river and stream
  Shall be crystal-clear and shall sparkle like wine,
  As if in a wondrous dream."

The Night of Wishes

And Tyrannia followed suit:

"O potent bowl of omnipotent potion,
  Now hear my wish and grant me a notion:
  Anyone caught dumping refuse and waste
  Into our pure drinking water,
  Shall of neither whiskey nor wine ever taste
  But rather be led to the slaughter."

Once more they filled their glasses to the brim with
the potion and hurriedly quaffed it down. This time the
aunt was first.

"O potent bowl of omnipotent potion,
  Now hear my wish and grant me a notion:
  All those caught peddling sealskin and tusks,
  Or flesh from the last of our whales,
  Shall no more make deals for thousands of bucks
  But populate thousands of jails."

And her nephew immediately came up with:

"O potent bowl of omnipotent potion,
  Now hear my wish and grant me a notion:
  No manner of fish, of fowl, or of beast
  Shall perish at the hands of man.
  From this untimely fate may they be released
  And live their lives as nature planned."

After they both had downed yet another glass, the sorcerer boomed:

"O potent bowl of omnipotent potion,
  Now hear my wish and grant me a notion:
  And the four seasons, the warm and the cold,
  Confused by our smog and pollution,
  Shall now revert to the order of old:
  A fitting and proper solution."

And after a moment's reflection, the witch chanted:

"O potent bowl of omnipotent potion,
  Now hear my wish and grant me a notion:
  Anyone caught shooting holes in the sky,
  While aiming for world record sales,
  Shall spend all his days in the back of a sty
  Braiding the other pigs' tails."

One more glass went bottoms up, and again the witch was quicker:

"O potent bowl of omnipotent potion,
  Now hear my wish and grant me a notion:
  Anyone caught the seeds of war sowing,
  Among peoples of different race,
  Shall notice a hole in his pocket a-growing
  And his gold vanish without a trace."

And soon thereafter, Preposteror intoned in a stentorian voice:

"O potent bowl of omnipotent potion,
Now hear my wish and grant me a notion:
From bottom to top shall the sea thrive with life,
Its carpet of oil rolled away.
May the ocean's creatures be freed from all strife,
Along with its shores and its bays."

While they were chugalugging and rhyming away, they had more and more trouble suppressing their giggles.

In their imaginations, they pictured the havoc being wreaked in the world by their seemingly oh so noble wishes, and it was a great thrill for them to so thoroughly bamboozle the two animals and thus their High Council. At least that's what they thought they were doing. On top of that, the effects of the alcohellish hooch were beginning to show more and more, as was to be expected. They were both pretty seasoned characters and could handle quite a bit, but the haste with which they were forced to drink combined with the devilish strength of the potion did its part.

Michael Ende

The longer they swaggered and blustered about, the
more grandiose and long-winded their wishes became.
After they had knocked back more than ten glasses
apiece, they started howling and roaring.

Tyrannia had just had her turn:

"O potent bowl of omnipotent potion,
  Now hear my wish and grant me a notion:
  The wealth that we boast of at home
  And acquire through other folks' need—hiccup!—
  Shall henceforth be earned on our own,
  Which should serve to bridle our greed."

After which Preposteror shouted:

"O potent bowl of omnipotent potion,
  Now hear my wish and grant me a notion:
  The dangerous sources of energy

The Night of Wishes

Shall all be banned—oops!—
While wind and sun shall be happily
At our command."

After the next glass, the witch shrieked:

"O potent bowl of omnipotent potion,
  Now hear my wish and grant me a notion:
  Solely things good and solid and real
  And born of man's labor and sense
  Shall be made objects of barters and deals,
  Not dignity, life, or conscience—hiccup!"

And the sorcerer bayed:

"O potent bowl of omnipotent potion,
  Now hear my wish and grant me a notion:
  No new pestilence, natural or fabricated,
  Shall plague animal- or mankind—oops!—
  And those that exist are hereby dissipated,
  For once out of sight, out of mind."

And once again each of them tossed down a brimming
glassful and Tyrannia screeched:

"O potent bowl of omnipotent potion,
  Now hear my wish and grant me a notion:
  Grace the children with joy and with health
  In a future world of milk and honey—oops!—
  May they know that there's much more to wealth
  Than squatting atop piles of money—hiccup!"

Preposteror countered with a rhyme of his own, and so it went on and on. It was a kind of Binge and Rhyme Competition in which first one, then the other, pulled ahead by a nose, but neither could leave the other behind in the stretch.

The raven and the cat were filled with fear and dread at what they saw and heard. After all, they had no way of checking the results of these wishes in the real world outside. Had that single, as yet inaudible note from the New Year's bells actually done its work? Or had it perhaps been too weak to cancel out the devilish reverse effect of the potion? What if the sorcerer and the witch were successful, after all, and the exact *opposite* of everything they wished came true? If so, the worst catastrophe the world had ever known was already underway and no one could stop it now.

Jacob Scribble had stuck his head under his wing, and Morris took turns blocking his ears, then his eyes, with his paws.

In the meantime, the witch and the sorcerer seemed gradually to be growing weary, partly because they were having more and more trouble finding rhymes and were sure they had long since more than fulfilled their contractual quota of evil deeds anyway—and partly because the joy had gone out of it for them. They also were unable to observe the actual results of their wishing magic with their own eyes, and people of their ilk are really happy only when they can bask directly in the misfortune they have conjured up.

That was why they now decided to have a few private laughs with the rest of the Notion Potion and conjure more in the immediate vicinity.

Jacob and Morris almost had heart attacks when they heard this. Now there were only two possibilities left: either Father New Year's bell tone hadn't worked, in which case the jig was up anyway, or it had indeed canceled out the reverse effect of the potion. This, of course, would not go unnoticed by Preposteror and Tyrannia. And it wasn't hard to guess what was in store for the cat and the raven then. They exchanged uneasy glances.

But Preposteror and Tyrannia had by then already hoisted more than thirty glasses each and were sloshed to the gills. They were barely able to stay on their chairs.

"Now listen, my dear—hiccup!—dear Tauntie Eye," the sorcerer slurred. "How's abous we take a crack at our llovely littl' lanimals. Wh . . . wh . . . whaddayathink?"

"Good idea, Bulzebeeba," said the witch. "C'mere, Jacob, my fresh, little sad s—hiccup!—of feathers!"

"Wait a minute!" croaked Jacob in dismay. "If you please, madam, not with me, no. I don't want to, help!"

He tried to flee, and tottered about the laboratory in search of a hiding place, but Tyrannia had already downed an entire glass and now uttered, not without difficulty, the following rhyme:

The Night of Wishes

"O potent bile of omnipitent pition,
  Now hear my wish—hiccup!—and grunt me a
    nition:
Jacob Scribble shall—oops!—at last find haven
From his pains, wounds, and rheumatism.
In their stead, see a fine-feathered ra . . . raven
And a most finely tuned organism—hiccup!"

The sorcerer and the witch—and even the pessimistic raven himself—had expected that the poor thing would be left stark naked, like a plucked rooster, and would sink to his knees bent over in pain, more dead than alive.

Instead, Jacob suddenly felt himself decked out with a wonderfully warm, shining, blue-black coat of feathers, more beautiful than he had ever had in his life. He ruffled his feathers, fluffed them up, puffed out his chest, spread first his left, then his right wing, and studied them with tilted head.

Both were impeccable.

"Well, break my yoke!" he rasped. "Morris, do you see what I see, or have I flipped my lid?"

"I see what you see," whispered the little cat, "and I congratulate you from the bottom of my heart. For an old raven you look almost elegant."

Jacob beat his brand-new wings vigorously and croaked with enthusiasm, "Hooray! My pains are all gone! I feel as if I had just been hatched!"

Preposteror and Tyrannia stared at the raven with

glassy eyes. Their brains were much too fogged over to really grasp what was happening.

"Wh . . . what's going on here?" muttered the witch. "Wh . . . what's that . . . hiccup! . . . crazy bird up to now? Th . . . that's all wrong."

"Aunnie Tootoot," giggled the sorcerer, "I guessh you bingled something—hiccup!— You're getting everything all mexed up! You're a littl' rusty, poor old girl. Lemme show you how a—oops!—profussional does it. Now watch this." He downed another frothy glassful and burbled:

"O putent pole of onnupotent lotion,
 Now wear my dish and grind me a motion:
 May this cat be majestic as no cat before,
 Sound of belly, of mind, and of throat—hiccup!—
 And the bist . . . bestest singer, the greatest tenor,
 With the woe-snightest . . . snow-whitest coat."

Morris, who had been deathly sick and hardly able to mutter a sound a moment before, suddenly felt his measly, fat, little body tautening, growing, and assuming the size of a picture-perfect, muscular tomcat. His fur was no longer full of silly-looking spots, but silky smooth and white as snow, and his whiskers would have put a tiger to shame.

He cleared his throat and said in a voice which suddenly sounded so rich and melodious that he himself was instantly enamored with it, "Jacob, my dear friend—how do I look?"

The raven winked at him and rasped, "High-class, Morris, strictly big-time. Just like you always wanted."

"You know, Jacob," said the cat, stroking his whiskers, "maybe you should call me Mauricio di Mauro from now on, after all. It suits me better, don't you think? Just listen!"

He took a deep breath and intoned a schmaltzy "*O sole mio . . .*"

"Shush!" said Jacob, and gestured to him to stop. "Be careful!"

But, fortunately, the sorcerer and the witch hadn't heard a thing, for a terrible fight had broken out between them. Each accused the other of having done something wrong, in a loud, drunken slur.

"You take yourself for a professional?" shrieked Tyrannia. "Don't make me laugh, ha, ha. You're nothing but a—hiccup!—ridiculoose amateur."

"How dare you!" Preposteror roared back. "You of all people want to slur my profussional refu . . . poopoo . . . reputation, you old hag of a dilettauntie."

"Come on, kitty," whispered Jacob. "I think we better beat it. They're going to catch on to us soon; then things will come to a bad end for us, after all."

"But I'd love to see how it ends," whispered the cat.

"Unfortunately, you don't have any more brains than you did before," said the raven. "Oh well, what does a singer need with brains? Come on now, hurry up!"

And while the sorcerer and the witch were still quarreling, the two of them stole undetected out through the broken window.

Only a small amount of the Notion Potion remained. The aunt and her nephew were already as drunk as skunks, if you'll pardon the expression. And, as is always the case when the blood alcohol level of such nasty characters reaches a hundred proof, they talked themselves more and more into a senseless fury.

They were no longer thinking of the animals, and thus happily did not notice their disappearance. They still had not hit on the idea that something could have canceled out the reverse effect of the magic potion. Instead, they each decided in their bottomless rage to let the other have it once and for all—this time with the power of the potion itself. Each intended to subject the other to the most evil and dastardly of all possible treatments. They wanted to conjure one another as old as

Methuselah, as ugly as sin, and straight to death's door. That is why they tossed down yet another full glass in unison, and screeched as with one voice:

"O pittant ball of umniputent potion,
  Now smear my fish and rant me an ocean:
  May you enjoy beauty and hee!—eternal yoo-hooth,
  Health and—hiccup!—virtue rain down from
    above.
  May your spirrit be cleansed of all h . . . hate an'
    untruth
  An' above all—oops!—your heart full of love."

And suddenly, to their complete bafflement, they found themselves sitting opposite one another—as young and beautiful as a prince and princess out of a fairy tale.

Tyrannia was speechless as she touched her slim figure (of course, her sulphurous-yellow evening gown now hung about her like a tent), and Preposteror ran his hands over his head and shouted, "Egads, whassat sprouting on my dainty little dome?—hiccup!— Wow, what a wonderful he . . . he . . . head of hair! Give me a cirror and a momb . . . I mean, a morror and a cimb . . . I mean, a mirror and a comb . . . that I may tame these wild locks."

Indeed, his previously bald skull was now covered with an unruly black mane. His aunt, on the other hand, had long golden-blond hair cascading down over her shoulders, like the fabled Lorelei, and when she touched her formerly ever so wrinkly face, she cried out, "My —hiccup!—skin is as smooth as a baby's bottom!"

And then they suddenly stopped talking and smiled admiringly at one another, quite as if they had just met for the very first time (which, in a sense, was the case, considering their current state).

Even though the Notion Potion had thoroughly transformed the two of them—not as they had intended, of course—something had remained the same, or rather, had intensified: their drunkenness. After all, no magic can break its own spell; it just won't work.

"Bull'seyebaby," stammered the aunt, "you really are a peetie-swie. Although I must say—hiccup!—you look much too double all of a sodden."

"Hold, ye maiden fair," babbled her nephew, "you must be a mirage, for alluvasudd'n you've got a halo or two. In any case, I worship you, dearest Rintintauntie. My soul has done an about-face. Hiccup! I feel so embellished, y'know? So sweet and loving beyond all measure . . ."

"I feel just the same," she said. "I feel so good allaway
down to the bottom of my heart, I could hog the whole
world . . ."

"Tyeziewyzie," Preposteror managed to enunciate,
"you are such a thoroughly delightly auntie, I must
make up with you forever and ever. Whadyasay, shall

we call each other by our first names from now on?"

"But my sweet little Beebee," she replied, "we've allaways called each other by our first names."

Preposteror nodded with a heavy head. "Too true, too true. You're so incredibly right onesh again. In that case, we'll drop the Mister and Missis from now on. So just call me . . . hiccup! . . . wha's my name, anywho?"

"Wh . . . wh . . . who cares," said Tyrannia. "Let's forget what usa be. We wanna start a new life, don' we? After all, we were both such . . . hiccup! . . . evil, nasty people."

The sorcerer began to blubber. "We sure were. Repulsive disgrossting fiends is what we were ! Oops! I'm so ashamed, Auntie."

Now his aunt started crying buckets herself. "Come to my virginal bosom, thou yoble nouth . . . hiccup! . . . thou noble youth! Evvything's gonna be different from now on. We'll both be sweet and kind, me to you an' you to me an' we two to evvyone."

Preposteror was racked with sobs. "Oh yes, oh yes, that's how it shall be! I'm so touched by us."

Tyrannia stroked his cheek and sniffed. "Don't cry so, my little turtle dove, you're breaking my hiccup. And besides, s'not even necessessary; we've already done so many good."

"When?" asked Preposteror, wiping the tears from his eyes.

"This evening, when do you think?" explained the witch.

"How so?"

"Because the potion granted all our wishes literally, understand? It didn't reverse anything."

"Howzyou know that?"

"Well," said the aunt, "just you take a looka us. Hiccup! Aren't we any proof?"

Only at that moment did she realize what she had just said. She stared at her nephew, and her nephew stared at her. He turned green in the face; she turned yellow.

"B . . . b . . . but that means," stuttered Preposteror, "we haven't fulfilled our contract in the least."

"And what is worse," whimpered Tyrannia, "we've even managed to gamble away everything we had to our credit beforehand. One hundred percent!"

"Then we're doomed!" roared Preposteror.

"Help!" screamed the witch. "I don't want to be foreclosed upon, I don't want to! Look, one m . . . m . . . more glass of potion is left for each of us. If we use it to wish something re . . . re . . . really bad, something really da . . . da . . . dastardly, maybe we can still save ourselves."

They both filled their glasses one last time as fast as they could. Preposteror even went so far as to lift the bowl of Cold Fire and shake out the very last drop. Then the two of them emptied their glasses with one gulp.

They started hemming and hawing and hemming and hawing, but neither of them could come up with a dastardly wish.

"It won't work," slobbered Preposteror. "I can't even put a curse on you, Tye."

"Me neither, Bubby," she wailed. "And do you know wh . . . wh . . . why? We're just *too darned good* now!"

"How horrible!" he lamented. "I wish . . . I wish . . . I was just like before, then all our plobrems would be solved."

"Me too, me too!" she sniveled.

And although it didn't rhyme, the Notion Potion

granted them this final wish as well. In one fell swoop they both became as they had been before: nasty-minded and highly displeasing to the eye.

But it was all in vain, for the Satanarchaeolidealcohellish Notion Potion had been drunk to the last drop. And the last glass finished them off. They fell off their chairs and lay sprawled on the floor.

At that very moment, a mighty bronze bell tone sounded from within the bowl of Cold Fire, shattering it to bits.

Outside, the New Year's bells began to chime.

"Ladies and gentlemen," said Mr. Maggot, suddenly seated in Preposteror's old armchair once again, "that's that. Your time is up. I am obliged to discharge the duties of my office. Do you have anything else to state by way of rejoinder?"

Snoring in two-part harmony was his only reply.

The visitor stood up and allowed his lidless gaze to

sweep through the devastated laboratory. "Well, well," he muttered, "we seem to have had quite a jolly time. I doubt that we will be in such a frolicsome mood upon awakening."

He lifted one of the glasses, sniffed it curiously, and shrank back in shock.

"Heaven's bells!" he said, throwing it down in dis-

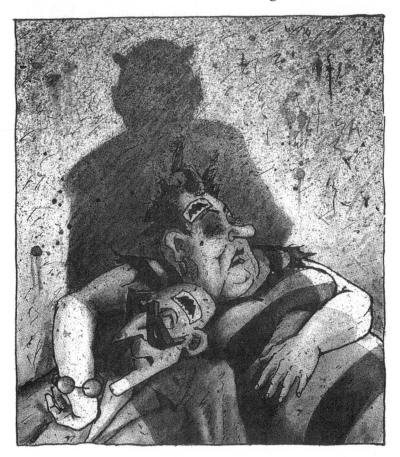

gust. "What a revolting aroma! I smell a rat, in more ways than one."

He shook his head and sighed. "And to think people drink such stuff! Oh well, there simply aren't any more connoisseurs nowadays. It really is high time that such incompetent riffraff be taken out of circulation."

With that, he reached into his black briefcase and withdrew a couple of bailiff's stamps bearing the likeness of a bat. He licked and carefully pasted them on the foreheads of Preposteror and Tyrannia. Each time there was a slight hiss.

Then Maledictus Maggot settled back down in the armchair, crossed his legs, and waited for the hellish soul shippers, who would soon come to carry them off. All the while he whistled a happy tune, for he was thinking contentedly of his impending promotion.

Meanwhile, Jacob Scribble and Mauricio di Mauro were sitting next to each other on the roof of the cathedral.

They had climbed up once again, which had been no trouble whatsoever given their newly found strength. Now they looked on happily as people exchanged hugs behind a thousand brightly lit windows and countless fireworks shot into the air, bursting into iridescent sheaves of fire above the town. And they listened, deeply moved, to the magnificent concert of the New Year's bells.

Father New Year, now a stone figure once more,

gazed down upon the festive glow from the heights of the steeple with an enraptured smile.

"Happy New Year, Jacob," said Mauricio with a choked voice.

"Same to you!" replied the raven. "All the best. Take care, Mauricio di Mauro."

"That sounds like a goodbye," said the cat.

"Yes," croaked Jacob hoarsely. "It's all for the best, believe me. When things have regained their natural order, then cats and birds will be natural enemies again."

"It's a pity, really," said Mauricio.

"Don't worry about it," said Jacob. "After all, that's the way things are."

They were silent for a while and listened to the bells.

"I wonder whatever became of the sorcerer and the witch," the cat said eventually. "I suppose we'll never know."

"Doesn't matter," said Jacob. "The main thing is that everything worked out well."

"Do you think so?" asked Mauricio.

"Sure!" rasped Jacob. "The danger is past. We ravens have a sixth sense about such things, and we're never wrong."

The cat pondered on it for a while. Then he said softly, "Somehow I almost feel sorry for the two of them."

The raven gave him a dirty look. "Oh, just be quiet!"

They both were silent and continued listening to the concert of the bells. They still didn't want to part.

"In any case," said Mauricio, breaking the silence once

again, "it is sure to be a very happy year for all—that is, if the rest of the world is as lucky as we were."

"No doubt about it." Jacob nodded meaningfully. "But the humans will never know who they owe their luck to."

"Certainly not the humans," the cat agreed, "and even if someone told them, they would think it was a fairy tale at best."

Another long pause ensued, but still neither one made any attempt to bid the other farewell. They gazed into the glittering, starry night, which appeared higher and more infinite to them than it ever had before.

"You see," said Jacob, "these are the ups of life you've been missing out on."

"Yes," said the cat emotionally, "so they are. From now on, I'll be able to melt the hearts of one and all, won't I?"

Jacob cast a quick sideways glance at the stately snow-white tomcat and said, "Cat hearts, in any case. I, for my part, will be satisfied to get back to Elvira's cozy little nest. Her eyes are going to pop out of her head when she sees me in my classy tux, all young and snappy."

He smoothed a couple of errant feathers carefully back into place with his beak.

"Elvira?" asked Mauricio. "Tell me the truth, how many wives do you have, anyway?"

The raven cleared his throat in embarrassment. "Well, you know, there's no relying on women. You have to get a good supply ahead of time, otherwise you're liable to be left out in the cold. And a traveling bird needs many a warm nest. But you're too young to understand that."

The cat feigned indignation. "I'll never understand such things!"

"Just you wait, Mr. Minnesinger," said Jacob dryly.

By and by, the sound of the bells died away. They sat next to each other in silence. Finally, Jacob suggested, "We should go and report to the High Council. After that each of us can go his own private way."

"Wait!" said Mauricio. "We can always go to the High Council later. Now I would like to sing my first song."

Jacob looked at him in horror. "I saw it coming," he croaked. "Who do you want to sing for, anyway? There's no audience here, and I'm completely unmusical, I am."

"I shall sing for Father New Year and in honor of the Great Tom in Kitty Heaven," said Mauricio.

"All right"—the raven shrugged his wings—"if you must. But are you really sure that someone up there is listening?"

"It's nothing you could understand, my friend," said the cat with dignity. "It's *over your head.*"

He quickly licked his silky snowy-white coat one more time, smoothed his imposing whiskers, struck a pose, and, while the raven listened patiently, albeit uncomprehendingly, started meowing his first and most beautiful aria to the starry sky above.

Michael Ende

And since, by some miracle, he could suddenly speak fluent Italian, he sang in his incomparably mellifluous Neapolitan cat's tenor:

"*Tutto è ben' quell' che finisce bene . . .*"

Which means in English:

ALL'S WELL THAT ENDS WELL.

MICHAEL ENDE (1929–1995) was born into an artistic family in Bavaria, Germany. As a young man during the Second World War, he joined the anti-Nazi resistance rather than enlist in the army, as his teenage classmates were then being required to do. After the war, he finished high school and enrolled in drama school, hoping for a career as a playwright and actor. For the next few years he worked in regional theater and wrote plays and cabaret scripts. He also met his future wife, the actor Ingeborg Hoffmann. Ende found surprise success with the 1960 publication of his first children's book, *Jim Button and Luke the Engine Driver*. He would go on to write many plays, essays, poems, and books—including *Momo* (1973) and *The Neverending Story* (1979)—which have been translated into more than forty languages and sold millions of copies around the world. He lived with his first wife in Italy for sixteen years until her death, and traveled extensively in Japan with his second wife, Mariko Satō, who was also his Japanese translator.

HEIKE SCHWARZBAUER and RICK TAKVORIAN have collaborated on two translations of books by the German literary critic and novelist Christa Wolf, *Accident: A Day's News* and *What Remains and Other Stories*.

REGINA KEHN has illustrated editions of *The Nutcracker and the Mouse King* and *Ali Baba and the Forty Thieves*, as well as books by Michael Ende, Daniil Kharms, Cornelia Funke, Otfried Preussler, and Franz Kafka, among others. She is based in Hamburg, Germany.

SELECTED TITLES IN THE
NEW YORK REVIEW CHILDREN'S COLLECTION

RUSSELL HOBAN AND QUENTIN BLAKE
The Marzipan Pig

ASTRID LINDGREN
Mio, My Son
Seacrow Island

NORMAN LINDSAY
The Magic Pudding

ERIC LINKLATER
The Wind on the Moon

JOHN MASEFIELD
The Box of Delights
The Midnight Folk

WILLIAM McCLEERY AND WARREN CHAPPELL
Wolf Story

JEAN MERRILL AND RONNI SOLBERT
The Pushcart War

E. NESBIT
The House of Arden

DANIEL PINKWATER
Lizard Music

OTFRIED PREUSSLER
Krabat & the Sorcerer's Mill
The Robber Hotzenplotz

CHRIS RASCHKA
The Doorman's Repose

BARBARA SLEIGH
Carbonel: The King of the Cats

E. C. SPYKMAN
Terrible, Horrible Edie

ANNA STAROBINETS
Catlantis

CATHERINE STORR
The Complete Polly and the Wolf

ALISON UTTLEY
A Traveller in Time

T. H. WHITE
Mistress Masham's Repose